His sneering smile enraged her

With a tremendous effort Vicki kept her voice level. "I don't know what your game is—"

"Oh, no game, I assure you." His smile had completely faded. "Let me make your situation absolutely clear to you. The people in the village are my responsibility, and anyone attempting to cheat or corrupt them—"

"But I didn't."

"—will be made aware by me that it is an extremely ill-advised thing to do."

"Your responsibility?" Exasperation mingled now with her fear. "This is the twentieth century not the fourteenth." Her voice crackled with frosty politeness as she asked, "What exactly is it that you want from me?"

He gave her a long appraising look. "Well, mademoiselle—that rather depends on you."

RACHEL FORD was born in Coventry, descended from a long line of Warwickshire farmers. She met her husband at Birmingham University, and he is now a principal lecturer in a polytechnic school. Rachel and her husband both taught school in the West Indies for several years after their marriage and have had fabulous holidays in Mexico, as well as unusual experiences in Venezuela and Ecuador during revolutions and coups! Their two daughters were born in England. After stints as a teacher and information guide, Rachel took up writing, which she really enjoys doing the most—first children's and girls' stories, and finally romance novels.

Books by Rachel Ford

HARLEQUIN PRESENTS

1160—A SHADOWED LOVE

HARLEQUIN ROMANCE

2913—CLOUDED PARADISE

RACHEL FORD

love's fugitive

Harlequin Books

TORONTO • NEW YORK • LONDON
AMSTERDAM • PARIS • SYDNEY • HAMBURG
STOCKHOLM • ATHENS • TOKYO • MILAN

Harlequin Presents first edition October 1990
ISBN 0-373-11304-8

Original hardcover edition published in 1989
by Mills & Boon Limited

Printed in U.S.A.

CHAPTER ONE

'JUNKIE!'

The voice, harsh with disgust, splintered the air just above her. She felt a large hand slide behind her head to jerk it roughly up from the pillow, then there was the same voice, deep, contemptuous, again. 'She's nothing but a worthless junkie.'

He was speaking in French . . . her whirling mind registered that much. But who, she wondered dreamily, was he talking about, this angry man? Whoever it was, she was drowned too deep in sleep to rouse herself.

The hand shifted its position, catching a clump of her hair in something—a signet ring?—and dragging it out by the roots. Then, as she winced and gave a tiny moan of pain, her head was released abruptly to fall back on to the sagging pillow. The bed creaked, and through the shifting, disorientating haze that enveloped her she was aware of someone sitting down beside her, a bulky body trapping her leg beneath the sheet.

'Mademoiselle.'

The imperious voice demanded some sort of reply. She opened her eyes, wincing again at the light which streamed mercilessly through the open shutters above her narrow bed. Against the brilliance, a dark shape was looming towards her, the outline of a man, though she could make out nothing of him beyond the thick black hair, its edges fringed with a golden halo where the sunlight caught it. She closed her eyes once more.

'Go 'way.' Her voice was strangely slurred. 'I'm trying to sleep.'

Her tongue was too large for her mouth and the words themselves seemed to stick to the dry roof of her mouth. She was already plunging back into that strange, uneasy oblivion when a pair of hands seized her by the shoulders and dragged her upright so that her head lolled helplessly.

'Mademoiselle.' That hated voice was in her ear again, no angelic cooing in spite of that sunshine halo, but curt, sharp with distaste. 'Wake up.'

A quick, angry shake accompanied the words and, caught off balance, she toppled over, to come up against something hard and unyielding. For a long moment she lay inert, the only sensation the man's rapid heartbeat under her cheek, then, above her head, she heard him give an impatient exclamation and say something in that quick, imperious voice. Next moment, someone was wiping her face with a wet cloth, so cold that it must surely have been wrung out in iced water. She caught her breath in a shuddering gasp and jerked back. Her eyes flew wide open and she stared up into the man's face, six inches from her own.

Her first impression was of sheer physical strength; her second, almost instantaneous, was of the total lack of any human warmth. That hard-planed face, the square, determined jaw, the thin mouth—they all showed arrogance, pride, toughness in plenty, but nothing of any redeeming softness. Even his eyes, though they were blue—like David's, she thought involuntarily—completely lacked the mild gentleness of his regard. Here—and though the room was full of stagnant heat she shivered suddenly—there was only the intense clarity of a sapphire, the blue-black, not of the sun-dappled surface of the sea, but of the icy depths miles beneath, where the finger of warming sunlight had never fallen.

She tried to speak, but during the night someone must have filled her mouth with dry, powdery ashes. 'I——'

The man regarded her with a look of cold interrogation and she ran her parched tongue around the outline of her dry lips. 'I don't feel well,' she muttered. 'C-can I have a drink of water, please?'

A tumbler was thrust into her hand, but her grasp was so unsteady that the glass chattered against her teeth and spilled over. She felt him take it from her and hold it, while she drained it greedily. Then, as she wiped the back of her hand shakily across her mouth, she became aware for the first time that behind the man a woman was standing, at the foot of the bed.

She looked from one to the other of the grim, unsmiling faces. 'Who—who are you?'

Her voice trembled slightly and she gazed past the man, unwilling to meet his eyes, to the woman. It was he who replied, though, speaking now in a barely accented English which did not mask the heavy sarcasm. 'Despite all your—endeavours, you have surely not forgotten that you have already met Madame Renant, the *patronne* of this *auberge*?'

Of course. Madame Renant... Memory was slowly seeping back into her confused mind. And yet yesterday she had been a jolly, smiling woman, for whom nothing was too much trouble, whereas now—— Suddenly, she was very frightened.

'I don't understand,' she said slowly. 'What's happened—and who are you, *monsieur*?'

'My name is Gilles Laroque. And you are Miss Victoria Summers of London, England—although that is of no account to me—or you—at present.'

Vicki gazed at him in bewilderment. How did he know her name? Of course—the hotel register. But his last words—they seemed to contain some barely concealed threat, which she could make no sense of at all but which none the less sent a shiver of inexplicable fear through her. But that was presumably exactly what he was aiming for, and she must not give him the cheap pleasure of seeing that he had succeeded in disturbing her even more.

For a long moment she forced herself to hold his gaze, but then his eyes travelled downwards, with a slow, deliberate insolence, and as she bent her head she realised that he was taking in, with unmistakable mockery, her white, fine lawn, shift-style nightie, the narrow straps accentuating her slim shoulders, the insets of white cotton-lace barely masking the curve of her delicately moulded breasts. She flushed, and his hands, still holding her upright, were suddenly burning into her skin so that she tried to draw away from him.

'Then I must ask you, Monsieur Laroque,' she stopped, struggling to subdue the unsteadiness of her voice and to infuse it with a spurious haughtiness, 'to leave my bedroom. You have no right——'

'No right, *mademoiselle*? On the contrary, you will find that I have every right. Jeanne here is a widow with four children. When she telephoned me this morning, in considerable distress, to tell me that three of her young foreign guests had left, silently, in the night, having—overlooked the courtesy of settling their account—well, as a fellow villager and long-time friend, how could I disregard her call?'

When Vicki stared up at him uncomprehendingly, he shook her again. 'Well? What do you say?' She remained silent, and he gave her a thin smile. 'And when she told me that the fourth member of the group, overcome no doubt by her excessive indulgence in drugs, was still lying here—well, I am sure you will agree, *mademoiselle*, that it was right for me to come at once?'

Foreign guests left . . . drugs . . . Vicki struggled desperately to filter some meaning from his words. But her head was aching—no, thumping—sickeningly, and her whole body felt as though it had been stretched for too long, like old, withered parchment, over a drum. Perhaps she had wandered into a madhouse—or perhaps, yes, that must be it, she was still dreaming. The whole night had been filled with dreams—vivid, disturbing, frightening dreams—and these two unsmiling people must merely be a continuation of those unnerving hallucinations.

And yet—the wetness on the front of her nightie where she had spilled some of the water felt clammily real, and those hands, gripping her so tightly now that she seemed to feel the bruises already springing up under the splayed fingers—these, surely, however much she might wish otherwise, were the stuff, not of dreams, but of cold reality . . .

'I—I don't know what you mean,' she whispered at last.

'Oh, it is very simple, *mademoiselle*.' Somehow, he made even this word into a subtle insult. 'When you arrived here three days ago with your—friends, Jeanne did not care much for the look of you all.' A dull flush crept up her cheek at the open taunt in his voice. 'But you had money, a hired car, so against her better judgement she allowed you to stay.

'Last night, she found an empty packet of amphetamines in the other young woman's room and intended asking you all to leave today. They forestalled her by some hours, however, but not without abandoning you in the casual manner I would expect from such—trash. Because you could not be woken from your drug-induced sleep——'

'No!' Vicki burst out wildly. She covered her ears against hearing any more. 'It's not true—not true, I tell you.' She was shaking now. 'It's all a mistake—a horrible mistake. You'll see. They've gone out for a walk—to the waterfall, that's where we were planning on going today. That's all—they'll be back, I swear it.'

His laugh was a sneer. 'Oh, yes, how foolish of me. They have merely gone for a stroll—to the waterfall, taking all their belongings—and the car with them, merely, of course, in case of fatigue.'

His biting words stunned her into silence. He was wrong, he had to be. Mike and the others—from the moment when she'd given them a lift on the outskirts of Carcassonne they'd been such fun, so carefree, lifting, for the first time in months, the shadows from around her heart. And when she'd told them that she was heading up into the Pyrenees and they'd said that they were going that way too, well, they didn't seem like hitch-hikers any longer—more like friends—and she'd been more than glad for them to come along.

But then, as her eyes wandered past the man's cold face to roam around the room, her gaze finally took in what her befuddled brain had been struggling to register since she had first painfully opened her eyes. A bed . . . a chest of drawers . . . a large, old-fashioned wardrobe—and nothing else.

Choking down the nausea that was rapidly threatening to overwhelm her, she threw back the bedclothes and swung her legs over the edge of the bed. A wave of dizziness hit her as she straightened up, but somehow she bit back the groan and, oblivious now of them both—and oblivious too of the brevity of her nightie—she tottered, first to the window where, leaning out, she saw with a sick misery that her hired car was no longer in the yard below, then across to the wardrobe, where she fumbled at the door and at last flung it open.

It was empty. Her neatly hung clothes had all gone, scooped off their metal hangers, no doubt, with a careless disregard for her sleeping a few feet away. She leaned up against the varnished wood and closed her eyes for a moment. Please, please let them not have taken it. But when, moving very stiffly and clumsily, she knelt in front of the chest and slid open the bottom drawer, her handbag too was gone, as she already knew it would be.

Everything had gone. They had left her literally with nothing but the clothes—this flimsy nightie—that she stood up in. Even as the hysterical laugh welled up inside her, though, the pain of their betrayal, the bitter knowledge that yet again her judgement had failed her, obliterated all other feelings. Well, you've never been particularly good at choosing friends—or anyone else, for that matter. So what's new? she thought with a self-lacerating twist of pain, and rested her head down on her arms.

Behind her, a derisive voice said, 'You're still full up with the filthy stuff, aren't you?'

Oh, why didn't he just leave her alone to die quietly? She shook her head in vehement denial. 'No.' Her voice was muffled against her arms. 'No, I'm not.'

The woman spoke, for the first time, in a clipped dialect which she could not follow. The man laughed scornfully and said in English, 'Jeanne has always been soft-hearted. She says you do not look like a drug addict—but we know better, *n'est-ce pas*?'

She heard a quick footstep, then his hands were beneath her arms, pulling her roughly to her feet. She clapped her hand to her mouth as churning sickness spiralled viciously inside her, then said against clenched teeth, 'Please, I feel sick.'

With a half-smothered expletive he put his arm round her waist, shouldered open the bedroom door and, as she feebly tried to push him away, half carried, half dragged her along the cord-carpeted passage to the small bathroom. In the doorway, overwhelmed by humiliation, she made one final, fruitless effort to shut the door in his face, then collapsed in a huddle over the lavatory, as the sickness tore at her insides.

After one particularly violent spasm, she managed to gasp out, 'Go away—please.'

'Certainly not.' His voice mocked her. 'After all, you might attempt to climb out of the window. Jeanne has lost three of you—I do not intend to lose the fourth.'

But the window was so small that nothing larger than a cat could have squeezed itself through. Helpless anger stirred in her. 'Oh, you—you go to hell.'

She just had time to hear him laugh softly, before her stomach was wrung inside out yet again. What on earth was wrong with her? She'd never felt like this before in her whole life. Food poisoning? But she'd eaten nothing that could have affected her so severely. Could it possibly be . . .? *Could* he be right? Could she have been drugged—not by her own hand, as he clearly believed, but by another's? Drained of everything but the intense desire to sink back again into nothingness, she laid her cheek against the welcome cold of the tiles, but he jerked her back to her feet once more.

As they regarded each other in the dim, greenish light, she realised for the first time just how enormous he was. Tall—the naked electric bulb was still swinging softly where it had come in contact with his head a moment before—and with broad, powerful shoulders. And it was not only his sheer physical size that all but filled the small room. He exuded a solid power, a feeling of rock-like strength that would, she thought, with faint wistfulness, be very comforting to snuggle up to. You could feel very safe with a man like——

Her grey eyes opened wide. What on earth was she thinking of? Snuggle up to this loathsome, arrogant man? The drugs which she now felt certain she had been pumped full of must have temporarily turned her brain, making her quite incapable of rational thought . . .

She felt herself becoming increasingly ill at ease under his narrow-eyed, dispassionate scrutiny. 'You look, *mademoiselle*,' he remarked at last, 'exactly like one of the pathetic skinned rabbits which my shepherds catch and prepare up in the high pastures.'

'Well, thank you.' She tried a shaky attempt at an ironic laugh.

'A pale, thin waif,' he went on, as though she hadn't spoken, 'fragile—so fragile that I could break you with one hand.' His grip tightened momentarily on her arm, but then, as she flinched away, his lips twisted and he drew out a handkerchief from the pocket of his denims and, with a gentleness which astonished her, wiped her clammy face.

She put her hand to her head, the dizziness from the drug redoubled all at once by the sudden touch of his warm, strong fingers.

'I—I must lie down,' she blurted out, and stumbled past him, back to the bedroom. But before she could crash down into oblivion once more, those strong hands caught her up again, this time lifting her right off the ground, so that she lay against him, smelling his warm maleness, her forehead against the soft blue cotton of his shirt, her toes brushing the floor like a limp marionette.

Across her head, a quickfire conversation went on in that same sharp-edged dialect, a one-sided conversation even to Vicki's uncomprehending ears. It was plain that Gilles Laroque was settling things entirely to his satisfaction, the woman putting in an occasional half-hearted and obviously unsuccessful protest.

At last, he turned towards the door, still with her in his arms, and through her half-closed eyes she saw Madame Renant put a restraining hand on his arm and appear to remonstrate with him, but then she shrugged helplessly and, picking up the cotton counterpane, tucked it around her. She did not smile, but something in the thoughtful, caring gesture made Vicki's eyes fill with tears of weakness. She closed her eyes quickly, then turned her head into his chest, as another wave of nausea made her senses reel horribly.

She felt herself being carried downstairs, then the morning sun was hot on her face. His footsteps echoed across the cobbled yard, then stopped, and when she opened her eyes they were alongside a battered old Land Rover.

'Can you sit up—or would you rather lie in the back? I feel I should warn you, though,' there was a faintly ironic note in his voice, 'I had sheep in there yesterday.'

Alarm bells were clamouring wildly, and she shook her head in a desperate effort to clear the dizziness. 'I'm not going with you.' Panic sharpened her voice, sending it up half an octave. 'Put me down, do you hear me? I won't go!'

He smiled down at her, not a particularly pleasant smile, which showed a row of strong white teeth. *I could break you with one hand.* 'You have just one alternative, *mademoiselle*. Either you get in of your own accord—or I throw you in.'

She stared up at him. The smile had faded, leaving his features set in tight lines. 'Where——' it was a croak '—where are you taking me?' A sudden, terrifying thought struck her. 'You're handing me over to the p-police, aren't you?'

This time he laughed out loud, but the expression in the ice-cold blue eyes only intensified her fear. 'Oh, no, *mademoiselle*. Do not be afraid. There is no need for us to trouble the police—in this village we settle our own affairs. No, I am merely taking you to my home.'

Taking her to his home? She gave a violent start and clutched the edges of the counterpane to her. Who knew what terrors lay behind those innocuous-sounding words? 'No—no, you're not. I won't go! Let me down, do you hear me?'

'I hear you perfectly.'

'Well, then, put me down.'

She tried to break free from his grasp, but his arms only tightened their hold on her. Her eyes roved frantically, seeking escape—or help—and she caught sight of Madame Renant still standing at the open door, a wide-eyed toddler now clinging to her skirt.

But, even as she opened her mouth to call to her, he said quickly, 'It is not the slightest use your appealing to Jeanne's goodness of heart. I am afraid I have persuaded her that as a widow with four young children she must not run the risk of your bringing drugs under her roof again.'

'Oh!' Vicki gasped, as though he had deluged her with more of that icy water. 'I'm not a drug addict, I tell you. I've never taken drugs.'

'Never, mademoiselle?' He raised his dark brows in mock interrogation, but she clamped her mouth on the angry retort that had sprung to her lips.

'You just won't understand, will you?' was all that she allowed herself to say. 'And now, as I refuse to go home with you, and as you can't make me——'

'Oh, but I can.' His voice was silky-soft, but the menace was there, like cold steel. 'You see, Mademoiselle Summers,' his tone was offhand now, as though he was suddenly bored with the whole proceeding, 'I own this village, and this valley. Oh, yes,' as her horrified eyes flew to his, 'and up here in the mountains I do—anything I wish. I have recompensed Jeanne for the not inconsiderable sum which is owed to her by you and your delightful friends. So, now, as you are clearly unable to recompense me in return, I—how can I put it delicately?—for the present, at least, I also own you.'

CHAPTER TWO

A TINY voice, from somewhere in the very back of Vicki's mind, was telling her that she should cry out in protest—or even laugh—at his preposterous words, but her brain was just too sluggish to respond, so that in the end she did not even struggle when he opened the door of the vehicle and eased her into the passenger seat.

She opened her eyes only once on the mercifully short journey. They were just negotiating a sharp hairpin bend on a narrow, rutted road, and she looked down at—nothing, or rather at the green handkerchief fields, and the red pantiled toytown roofs of the village far below. Her stomach turned over, she gave a faint groan and hastily closed her eyes again, though not before she had seen the man beside her remove his gaze from the tortuous road just long enough to shoot her a swift glance, a grim smile flickering across his otherwise impassive features.

The swine. He knew exactly how she was feeling, and was enjoying every moment of it. Wearily she laid her head against the hard metal side of the vehicle as the spiralling dizziness hurtled her into semi-consciousness again.

As she was lifted out, she roused slightly with a whimper of protest and half opened one eye. Out of the shifting mists, a face was bending over her—a face, harsh and stern, that she knew she should recognise, and yet she couldn't quite remember where she'd encountered it before. She tried to speak, but her voice was slurred—she could hear it in her own ears—and her brain too was fuzzing up, like the fur inside a kettle. I'm turning into a kettle, was her last remotely coherent thought as she keeled over into a black gulf of sleep.

She opened her eyes to a room she had never seen before—white-walled, high-ceilinged, with heavy, old-fashioned furniture. The smell of lavender hung faintly in the air, and at first Vicki thought that this was just another part of the endless procession of strange, compelling dreams which had flitted through her unconscious mind, but when she turned her head she realised first that that subtle aroma of lavender was drifting from the cool pillow, second that she was awake, and third that a figure was standing over by the unshuttered window, his bulky form sharply outlined against the brilliant lozenge of golden light.

She half raised herself, but then, as the dreadful recollections tumbled pell-mell back into her mind, she fell back weakly on the pillow with a silent inner groan of misery. At the slight movement the figure, now all too horribly familiar, straightened up from where he had been leaning, arms folded, against the window-frame, and came over to stare down at her in a narrow-eyed scrutiny.

Vicki shrank down further into the bed as fear, shame, and downright panic struggled for supremacy inside her. How could Mike and his friends have done this to her? The drug—whatever it was—must have been in that last, bitter-tasting liqueur they'd laughingly forced on her last night. But why had they done it? Had they planned it all along, ever since she'd picked them up, or was it simply a spur of the moment trick? Either way—whatever was she going to do? No money, no car—nothing, while at the same time fate had delivered her utterly into the mercy of this man, who was even now regarding her very much as though mercy was going to be a considerable way down his list of priorities . . .

The panic won. Somehow she had to get away, now. With a convulsive jerk, she flung back the bedclothes, then caught sight of her skimpy white nightie, drawn up to the top of her tanned thighs. And at this moment this was all that she possessed in the whole world! The total, utterly forlorn helplessness of her situation hit her, like a savage physical blow, squarely in her midriff. With an impulsive gesture she dragged up the bedclothes again, lay down and curled on to her side away from him, as black misery engulfed her.

'So you are awake, *mademoiselle*.'

In spite of herself, she tensed at that hateful voice.

'No, I'm not. Just go away, will you?' she mumbled against the pillow, but then a terrified gasp was torn from her as he bent down and, catching her by the shoulder, wrenched her up into a sitting position, so that they stared at each other, he furious, she attempting fury but succeeding only in feeling even greater spasms of panic. Still, she knew instinctively that she must somehow try to hold her ground against him.

'Look, *monsieur*,' she began, shutting her ears to the faint uncertainty that hovered in her voice, 'don't try to bully me, or you'll be sorry, I promise you. It's time you realised that this ridiculous charade has got to end, so——'

'Oh, so the little skinned rabbit is attempting to flex her claws on me, is she?'

His sneering smile enraged her, but she knew that she had to hold on to her temper. With a tremendous effort, she kept her voice level. 'I don't know what your game is——'

'Oh, no game, I assure you.' The smile had completely faded. 'Now that you have had several hours' sleep and appear to be in a slightly fitter condition to listen, let me make your situation absolutely clear to you. The people in the village below are my responsibility, and anyone who attempts to cheat or corrupt them——'

'But I didn't! You must understand——'

'—will be made fully aware, by me, that it is an extremely—ill-advised thing to do.'

Exasperation mingled now with her fear, and all sensible thoughts of discretion disappeared rapidly through the window. 'For heaven's sake! *Your* responsibility? You're in the wrong century. Down there, outside your precious valley, it's the twentieth century, not the fourteenth. Feudalism, the benevolent father-figure who knows what's best for his people——' his dark brows came down in a snapping frown but the injudicious words tumbled out '—and heaven help them if they should ever begin to think that they know better. That's been gone a very long time, in case you hadn't noticed, and you're just being——'

'Be quiet, *mademoiselle*.' The icy voice was perfectly controlled, but it conveyed perfectly what he might unleash on her if provoked any further, and she stopped dead.

'I say again,' he went on, still in that chill tone, 'this valley is mine, and everything that happens in it is of great consequence to me. You will be wise to remember that.'

His fingers dug painfully into her shoulders for an instant, then he dropped his hands and they regarded one another across the white counterpane, he impassive apart from the faint flush which her hasty words had brought to his cheeks, she in mutinous if apprehensive silence. He just couldn't keep her here, a prisoner, against her will. Absolutely not—the whole idea was quite ridiculous. And yet—under the bedclothes her fingers clenched involuntarily—there was nothing even remotely ridiculous about this man. Uncompromisingly solid and hard, he had, she sensed, a strength and power that went far beyond the merely physical. The level, calculating, indigo eyes, the firm set of his mouth, the proud—no, *arrogant* way he had of carrying his head on those massive shoulders, all denoted a feeling of complete rightness, an inner strength, a completely inviolable sense that he was—who he was...

She tried to return his stare unflinchingly, but behind her pale forehead her mind, swept almost clean now of the immense amount of whatever drug they had used on her, was racing in something approaching overdrive. She had been stupid, allowing herself the luxury of getting so worked up. Anger would never succeed against a man like this—not that she had ever actually met a man like this before, she thought grimly, but all the same she knew she would need other, more subtle means than open hostility to fight him.

One thing she had to keep reminding herself of—she couldn't be kept here against her will. It was bluff. With such things as cars, planes, British consuls with money . . . and temporary passports . . . and tickets to freedom—no, it was sheer bluff. And yet Vicki could find little comfort in hugging that thought to her, for somehow he had managed to imbue his coolly spoken words with such assurance that it was impossible simply to shrug them off. Still, she told herself stoutly, she would play his game and somehow—she wasn't sure how yet—she would win, and shake the dust of this valley off her feet forever while Monsieur Gilles Laroque was still wondering what had hit him.

It would perhaps be best to begin by bringing his thinly veiled threats into the open. She would at least know then what she was fighting against. 'Could you perhaps enlighten me,' she said, her voice crackling with frosty politeness, 'on what exactly it is you want from me?'

He gave her a long, appraising look. 'Well, *mademoiselle*—that rather depends on you.'

Her shallow composure shattered instantly. 'W-what do you mean by that?' she demanded huskily.

'I have reimbursed Jeanne this morning. The four of you appear to have lived in a manner more befitting the medieval lords you accused me of being.' She looked at him suspiciously, almost certain that she had heard an undercurrent of irony in his voice, but his face held not the faintest hint of humour. 'And so,' he shrugged expressively, 'as your companions are absent—well, I am afraid the reckoning has been left for you to settle. Of course, if you have the money, I shall be delighted to accept it.'

'You know I haven't, damn you!' she burst out. 'You know that they've stolen everything.' In spite of her efforts, her voice shook slightly at the bitter reminder of their so-casual betrayal.

'Ah, but I only have your word for that, *mademoiselle*. The way I see it is somewhat different. You too were doubtless intending to slip away, but from negligence—or necessity—you took a larger dose than you were accustomed to, and your friends, unable to rouse you, were forced to leave you behind.'

'I've told you already, that's not the way it was,' she said tonelessly. What was the use? 'But in any case, even if you don't believe me, all this——' she spread her hands wide in an impatient gesture '—and over a few hundred francs. It's crazy.'

'To you it may be a few hundred francs, as you term it,' there was no mistaking the hardness in his tone now, 'but it is a livelihood or poverty to Jeanne and all the other people whom you no doubt planned to cheat.'

Her forehead was beginning to throb. She pressed the fingers of one hand to it, and tried again. 'Look, let me go home, and I promise you I'll send you the money straight away. If you release me today, I could get it to you—— ' she frowned in concentration '—oh, by Friday, I'm sure. You have my word. I'll——'

His lip curled. 'Your word? No, *mademoiselle*, you will repay me, but not from England, I assure you. I hold you in pawn here,' he gave her a thin smile, 'and, like any good pawnbroker, I intend to take very great care of my new acquisition until the debt has been wholly redeemed.'

Behind his words there was that threat again, still unspoken but all the more menacing for not being spelled out. It hung almost palpably in the air, as though weaving itself insidiously around her, and Vicki suddenly shivered.

She was gathering herself to make some sort of reply when there was a knock at the door and a young, rather scraggy girl in a blue overall came in, carrying an armful of clothes. She sidled timidly past them, shooting her, Vicki thought resentfully, the sort of look she would have bestowed on some six-headed monster with slavering fangs. Laroque exchanged a few words with her in that incomprehensible patois, then ushered her out with a reassuring smile which instantly, though fleetingly, transformed his bleak face.

He turned back to Vicki, the last vestiges of the smile disappearing. 'You understood what Monique said?'

She shook her head. 'No.'

'And yet you speak French very well.'

'I had a good teacher,' she said woodenly. The dull ache was travelling rapidly down from her head to her neck and shoulders. Perhaps she was allergic to pig-headed autocrats—yes, very likely that was it.

'Her mother has very kindly sent you some clothes. You cannot spend the rest of your life in that night-dress——' his opaque dark blue eyes skimmed across her shoulders in a cool, deliberate glance which brought the hot colour sizzling into her cheeks '—however revealing of your charms it may be.'

That provocative glance had thrown her totally off balance. 'Oh, so I'm supposed to be grateful,' she snapped, injecting an unwonted acidity into her voice.

He frowned and his lips tightened. 'I trust so, *mademoiselle*. They belonged to Monique's elder sister, who died recently in childbirth.'

Vicki stared at him mutely, then turned her head away abruptly. Whatever was happening to her? she wondered dully. This horrible, endless, wide-awake nightmare must be taking her over, infiltrating its own poison, even more potent than the drug, and subjecting her to a total personality change.

'I—I'm sorry. Tell her—Monique—to please thank her m-mother.'

To her horror, she felt her eyelids prickling, then scalding tears brimmed in her eyes and one overflowed, to race down her cheek before she could stop it. Keeping her head turned away, she bit on her lip hard. She heard him cross the room, then out of the extreme corner of her eye saw him standing over her. Even as she flinched further away from him she almost thought that, for a fraction of a second, his hand brushed against her bent head, but the impression was so fleeting that she knew she had imagined it.

'You are still weak,' he said brusquely. 'It is the effect of those filthy drugs. One of the maids will bring you a light lunch, which you must eat.' *Eat!* Her stomach churned anew at the very thought. Surely she'd never be able to face food again? He glanced at his watch. 'Now I must go, but I shall see you later.' And, before she could even begin to wonder if she should bridle at the domineering tone, he was gone.

She listened as his footsteps retreated along the passage then went swiftly down the stairs. For such a big man he moved amazingly lightly, she thought inconsequentially. Like a cat. No. A tiny fragment of fear fell into her mind like a droplet of ice-cold water. Not a cat—a stalking, thoroughly dangerous panther. And, just as a cat would play with a ball of wool or—she shuddered—a hapless mouse that had fallen into its grasp, so he was playing some private game with her.

She had to get away! But even as she hurled back the bedclothes and went to leap out of bed the furniture in the room dipped and swayed around her, and she sank back, feeling the clammy sweat break out on her forehead again. Perhaps he was right. Like it or not, her body needed food, and even if she did manage to get out of the house unnoticed she would almost certainly collapse in a heap before she reached the first bend of that mountain road.

Somewhere below, a door banged. Vicki got up very slowly and went over to the window, then drew back with an involuntary start. Laroque was almost directly beneath her, so that his true height was distorted and his shoulders and back appeared even more powerfully made, the muscles straining against the pale blue working shirt. As she watched, he climbed into the Land Rover, reversed, then shot away in a little flurry of gravel, lifting a suntanned hand in casual greeting to an elderly man in blue overalls who was raking the drive.

She watched for as long as the vehicle was in sight on the winding road, and only when it had quite disappeared did she become aware of the astonishing view. The house must be well up the mountainside, she judged, for beyond the tree-lined lawn, its sweeping lines broken by formal flower-beds enclosed in low box hedging and an ornamental, water-lilied pool, the ground dropped steeply away almost to a ravine. Miles below, or so it seemed, clasped as though by loving arms within the green embracc of the foothills of the Pyrenees, was the church, Jeanne's *auberge*, and the other houses which made up Gilles Laroque's precious village, while on the outskirts, she could just make out the sprawling range of clean, modern factory buildings which she had noticed when she had been driving around with Mike.

Mike. So carefree, so happy-go-lucky. He'd made her laugh more than she'd remembered doing for years, reducing her frequently to helpless giggles. A secret hope had even begun to form in her that maybe, back in England, he might be her way to a whole new beginning... Her lips twisted on an all-too-familiar stab of anguish. She straightened up abruptly and went through to the bathroom that led directly off her room.

The bedroom furniture was solid and old-fashioned but, even to her unschooled eye, redolent of money. The bathroom, though, was luxuriously modern, its ivory-embossed tiles exactly toning with the suite which had—she pursed her lips in a soundless whistle—a wealth of heavy-looking, gold-plated fittings.

She leaned against the basin and surveyed herself in the mirror, impersonally and without enthusiasm. Her dark chestnut-brown hair, normally sleek and well-groomed, hung on her shoulders in lifeless seaweed strands. Her face, a classic oval, usually softly rose-flushed, was completely transparent, colourless apart from the freckles brushed across her cheeks and the sooty smudges beneath her wide-set, long-lashed grey eyes. Her cheekbone structure, merely delicate just two days ago, had now developed an alarming and unbecoming hollowness.

Vicki stared pensively at the ghostly apparition, then suddenly and quite unexpectedly grinned at it. 'You look, my girl,' she said to herself severely, 'just like a consumptive poet who's about to hand in her dinner pail.' And with this salutory thought she peeled off her nightie, hesitated, then carefully locked the door and stepped into the shower, letting it cascade in a delicious warm stream over her hair and body. In the ivory porcelain shell dish there was a cake of Roger et Gallet soap—jasmine, her favourite—and she undid its paper wrapper, luxuriating in its delicate rich perfume, then lathered herself freely until she felt thoroughly cleansed.

On the shelf, alongside a new toothbrush and tube of paste, stood an unopened bottle of shampoo. Someone, aware of her complete lack of the everyday necessities that any ordinary house-guest would bring with them—and rarely could there have been a less ordinary, more unlikely, more unwilling house-guest, she reflected wryly—had thoughtfully provided these items. Not Laroque, surely, for he had displayed a singular lack of awareness of the gentlemanly niceties of civilised behaviour. A housekeeper, presumably, or—her hand jerked so that a trickle of shampoo ran down almost unnoticed into her eyes—more likely Laroque's wife, for surely a man in his position and of his age—middle thirties, she judged, and no doubt, in some women's eyes, an extremely handsome brute, though certainly not to her—must somewhere along the line have acquired a wife...

She blotted her hair rather absent-mindedly, briskly towelled her body, then went back to the bedroom. Among the pile of simple but immaculately washed and ironed clothes on the bed was a black and white skirt and a short-sleeved white cotton blouse. She put on a pair of pants, then climbed into the skirt, noticing with a grimace how, even with an elasticated waist, it hung on her slight frame. She'd been steadily losing weight for months, she knew that, but somehow she'd been able to shrug off the fact until now. Oh, well, slenderness was always fashionable, but even so, when she got home—when she finally got home, she amended—she must try somehow to put on a little weight. It would have to be peanut butter sandwiches and banana and ice-cream milkshakes once again.

She pulled one of the big, tapestry-covered armchairs over to the window and curled up in it to let the warmth dry her hair. The sun was high in the sky—it must be around noon, she judged, though she could not be sure for, like everything else, her watch had been stripped from her. She leaned back comfortably in the chair, the sun full on her closed eyelids, enjoying the pleasant, mind-easing sensation. It was almost as though she was drifting in a boat with no oars. She yawned hugely. It was tempting to let the current gently take her to what far shore it would...

She sat bolt upright as her eyes flew open. Was she insane? Drifting happily with the current...? She must get out of this place, and quickly. She was feeling stronger now; Laroque was safely, if temporarily, out of the way. So what on earth was she waiting for?

But even as she tensed to spring to her feet there was a soft knock, and a young lad, wearing neat denim trousers and jacket—and exactly the same wary expression, Vicki noticed with irritated amusement—came in with a tray. Without a word, he set it down on the side table and hastily retreated.

She stared at the door panels, then gave a rueful little shrug. Oh well, if they were all so determined to treat her like a pariah, that would only stiffen her resolve to escape. But just now there were clearly too many people around. After lunch, perhaps, things would quieten down, and then she would seize her chance.

She fetched the tray across and balanced it on her knees. Bread, butter, a glass of chilled white wine, which she left untouched, a feathery-light golden omelette gleaming with melted butter, and a slice of apricot tart. Well, at least her reluctant host did not intend to starve her... Vicki had not known just how hungry she was until, chasing the last few crumbs of tart around her plate, she registered the almost indecent haste with which she had eaten.

Her coffee arrived via another maid, older than Monique. Vicki smiled determinedly at her. 'Thank you. And also for the toiletries—will you please thank Madame Laroque?'

Her words caught her by surprise, seeming to come from her of their own volition, and the maid gazed back at her, equally surprised.

'But *mademoiselle*, Madame Laroque——' she hesitated '—there is no Madame Laroque. Monsieur Gilles told us to do it.'

As Vicki stared at her, she nodded and went out, quietly closing the door. Vicki's brow furrowed slightly. No Madame Laroque... So he wasn't married, after all... Thoughtfully she poured cream into the cup and sipped the strong, aromatic coffee. What an immense household it seemed to be—she'd encountered three servants already, all of them seemingly queuing up to view her, this monster from the outside world. Presumably, without a wife to cushion his domestic affairs, he needed so many servants—to satisfy his every need...

Abruptly Vicki set down her cup, the blood ebbing swiftly away from her face as she felt a *frisson* of real fear prickle up and down her spine. Just how naïve—not to say dim-witted—could she get? The drugs must have addled her brain totally. In spite of the unmistakable seriousness of his threats, she had comfortingly assumed—or at least managed to persuade herself—that, rather in the manner of Laurel and Hardy set to wash up mountains of dirty dishes in a restaurant when they could not pay the bill, so her captor intended her to pay off her account up to her elbows in greasy suds in his kitchen or on hands and knees scrubbing every doorstep.

But that, she knew now with sudden, frightening clarity, had been a wholly misplaced supposition. He had more than enough servants for such menial tasks already. So in that case—what was it he wanted from her? *I shall hold you in pawn here... until the debt has been wholly redeemed...* She was absolutely sure now of what it was that he would require in recompense—something which she was not, under any circumstances, prepared to give. And yet—she swallowed hard—would she be able to prevent him? He'd behaved ever since they'd met as if he were some feudal overlord, boasting that in this remote valley he was above all civilised law. Surely he couldn't possibly still practise here that infamous, medieval *droit de seigneur* on any young woman who was unfortunate enough to fall into his clutches?

Panic rose in her, blotting out all rational thought, and impulsively she leapt to her feet, crossed to the door and opened it. The house was utterly still now, wrapped in the hot, languid silence of early afternoon. She tiptoed back to the window and looked out; the grounds, the drive, the winding road, all were basking undisturbed in the heat haze. Perhaps it was now or never.

Among the clothes Monique had brought was a pair of floppy pink plastic sandals. She snatched them up and, her heart beating wildly, sped swiftly and silently down the broad staircase, framing in her mind some specious excuse about needing a little air. But no excuse was required; the huge, marble-flagged hall was deserted and no sound came to her. The door stood ajar, she was through it and already racing away down the drive before she realised that she had forgotten to put on her sandals.

She stopped to squeeze her feet into them, then ran on, stumbling in her haste, until she reached the entrance gates. She risked one quick glance over her shoulder, but no one was haring after her. The house—her eyes widened involuntarily as she took in its huge proportions—was quite undisturbed. Next moment, she was out of sight round a clump of trees and hurrying down the narrow, twisting road.

She could have hugged herself with relief. She'd got away—and, after all her fears, it had been so ridiculously easy. All she had to do was get through the village and she would be out of this horrible valley forever. True, she had no money, not one franc, but when she reached the main road she would hitch a lift to the nearest *gendarmerie* or, better still, British consul—in Toulouse, probably—and her nightmare would be over.

When she got home, she would immediately send him a money order, of course, which would more than cover the bill, but would accompany it with a letter—short, pithy and very much to the point. In the meantime, though, she would be very glad when she was past the village—*his* village—for an uncomfortable, tingling feeling on the nape of her neck was making her, in spite of her new-found confidence, cast hurried glances over her shoulder at the deserted road behind her.

The village was just ahead now. She hung back momentarily, chewing her lip as she scanned the cottages with their wide overhanging gables for any movement. But the shutters were all closed tightly against the heat, the only sound raucous music from behind one of the closed-up windows. The one sign of life was a mongrel dog, which gave a very half-hearted bark when it saw her, then yawned and went back to rooting out its fleas.

Once past the church, constructed, as so many in this region, like a miniature fortress, with massive castellated walls and tiny arrow-slit windows, the road curved away towards orchards and tree-lined meadows. As she rounded a bend which took her out of sight of the still-slumbering village, she let out her breath in a sigh of pure relief. Freedom. All his threats, his so thinly veiled innuendoes, had proved to be merely empty words. How foolish he would feel—and look—when her escape was finally noticed.

From the other side of the stone wall several huge, cream-coloured cows were eyeing her curiously and Vicki chirruped cheerfully at them. But then her confident stride faltered. Leaning against a white gate a few yards ahead were two young men. The uneasiness which had flickered in her stomach mounted rapidly to panic as they slowly straightened up and stepped out in front of her.

'Bonjour, messieurs.'

Somehow she put together a dazzling smile, but as she went to pass them one put a firm though perfectly gentle hand on her arm, and instantly, even as her heart plummeted to those tight pink sandals, she understood. There was not even any curiosity in those two pairs of brown eyes—they were merely doing exactly as they had been ordered.

'Monsieur Laroque was afraid that you will get lost if you stray too far,' one said, in very careful English. 'You must permit us to accompany you back to the village.'

Rage kindled lightning-swift in her, so that for an instant she had the urge to fall on the ground and beat her fists in frustration on the dusty road. But the rage evaporated just as swiftly, leaving her with a feeling of utter, paralysing helplessness, so that, when they gestured courteously towards the way she had come, she just nodded and turned back, leaving them to fall in on each side of her.

As the silent little group reached the square in front of the church, she heard behind them a vehicle, travelling at high speed. When it pulled up smartly, just alongside them, Vicki stopped but stared straight ahead, not deigning to turn to face the driver. A door slammed, footsteps crunched, and a moment later Gilles Laroque was standing before her.

CHAPTER THREE

VICKI sneaked one glance up at him from beneath her lashes, then stood, her head bent, sullenly kicking at a tuft of withered grass. When he put his hand firmly on her arm she did not even attempt to resist, but allowed herself, as though mesmerised, to be led across to the Land Rover. Only when he put his other hand on the passenger door did she manage to pull herself together to make one last effort.

'Please—no,' she whispered unsteadily, and met his ink-dark eyes beseechingly.

For a moment, she almost thought he hesitated, but then the split-second softening of those hard eyes vanished and he opened the door abruptly.

'Get in.'

As he swung himself in beside her and started the engine, he said, without even looking at her, 'I trust you now accept that it is futile to try to leave before I permit it. You have—obligations here, and I shall ensure that you fulfil them.'

She set her teeth on any response and instead turned her head away to stare fixedly out of the window as they made the now all-too-short return journey. Of course, all this had been set up—too late, she could see that now. He'd known that she would try to escape, had set the trap, and she had walked neatly into it. And her childish attempt to get away had merely enabled him to show her, with brutal clarity, that his threats, far from being empty, were all too real. A feeling of utter impotence engulfed her, and she clenched her hands in her lap until the bones of her knuckles stood out white.

As they pulled into the drive, she shot him a furtive glance. What was going on behind that hard profile? She had no idea. He seemed able to read her mind with perfect ease, to anticipate her every move, and yet, for her, there was no corresponding telepathy—he was a total enigma...

Almost before he had drawn up at the front entrance her fingers were fumbling with the door-catch, but too late. He reached across, put a large, detaining hand over hers and pulled it free.

'Not quite yet, *mademoiselle*. Let me just reassure myself that you have indeed learnt your lesson. You are a young, unmarried girl——' he did not seem to register the start she gave, and she made no effort to put him right '—who has already shown that she is quite incapable of managing her own affairs responsibly and who should therefore not wander the countryside alone——' a note of unmistakable irony had now entered his level, unhurried voice '—for I regret that not all my fellow countrymen are as chivalrous as I.'

'*You*—chivalrous?' The scornful response leapt from her before she could close her mouth tight against it. But when she looked at him she saw that her retort had failed to evoke in him anything more than a faint amused quirk at one corner of his thin lips. Anger flared in her—he was so sure of himself, and so clearly determined to get the last ounce of pleasure from her helplessness—but she forced it down and made herself turn to face him squarely.

'Now look, Monsieur Laroque. Once and for all, will you kindly tell me just how long you intend to——' she was about to say, keep up this foolish game, but sensibly substituted '—keep me here? I—I'm not on holiday. I'm—I was working, and I have to get back to London soon. You must please understand that.'

She looked at him hopefully, but he merely raised his shoulders in one of those ultra-expressive, ultra-Gallic shrugs, conveying infinite regret and yet at the same time, she realised with a sick chill, meaning absolutely nothing. All her arguments, her insults, her pleas, were like the useless flutterings of a bird trapped in his hands, and sitting here beside him she could feel the tension tightening around her, notch by infinitesimal notch, until it seemed that she must surely explode with the inflammable mix of fear and anger.

In an effort to calm herself she uncurled her fingers, feeling as she did so the pain where the nails had bitten into her palm, and laid them, fingers outspread, in her lap. 'Please tell me,' she said in a low, toneless voice, 'what it is you intend for me.'

'Oh, I am sure, Victoria,' his tone had dropped to an insinuating purr, 'that we can come to some arrangement which is—*convenable* to both of us.' A lock of silky, newly washed hair was hanging by her cheek, and very gently, his skin hardly grazing hers, he lifted it with one finger and tucked it behind her ear. 'After all, now that you have lost that appearance of a badly skinned rabbit, I see that you are a very attractive young woman.'

That finger, with a delicacy she would not have believed possible, was lightly outlining the shell curve of her ear. Hardly knowing what she was doing, Vicki half closed her eyes as, pausing over the lobe, he lightly brushed against it, then slid the back of his thumb down the side of her neck and under the white collar of her blouse to rest against the soft skin of her shoulder. What magic gentleness there was in his touch. She gave a little sigh of pleasure and leaned back into the hard seat, all her tensions relaxing under those caressing fingers, then felt herself sway slightly towards him——

Her eyes jerked open. What lunacy was possessing her now? There could not be the faintest doubt any longer of how Laroque intended to redeem his debt and, with her response, she could not blame him if he now thought that there would be no obstacle to the fulfilment of that payment. She snatched at the door-handle, almost fell out on to the drive and propelled her unsteady legs through the deserted hall and up the wide staircase.

She slammed the door behind her and leaned against the comforting solidity of the panelled wood. Safe at last! She could have laughed out loud as the trite, empty thought sprang into her mind. Safe? You little fool, she thought sombrely; you aren't safe anywhere in this house.

Her tautly held body, exhausted by the tensions of the last hour, was threatening to crumple under her; she took the few steps to the bed and collapsed full-length on to it, hoping to escape into sleep. But this time her restless mind refused to give her oblivion and instead she lay, her hand to the side of her face, feeling her skin still tingle as though from sunburn where his light touch had brushed so sensuously across it, leaving a trail of warm consciousness. It was almost, she thought with a shiver, as though he had been testing her reactions, and that little secret smile which she had glimpsed just as she plunged out of the Land Rover showed that her treacherous body had surely given him the answer he sought.

Somehow, she must convince him that, despite his overweening male arrogance, he was wrong. But if she tried to resist him would that only mean that, with his superior strength, he would take her by force? Her mouth went dry with apprehension, but even in her fear she found her thoughts straying to what it would be like to be made love to by this man, so strong, so powerfully built and yet, it seemed, capable of such seductive gentleness. He would, she was sure, be a skilled, practised lover, in such contrast with her own inexperience... The unpleasant thoughts and the long-buried images rose in her like the slow bubbles on the surface of a stagnant pond, and she turned her head, stifling the little moan in her pillow.

When at last someone knocked at the door, her whole body tensed and she had to steel herself to call, 'Come in.'

It was only Monique, though. '*Monsieur* says you are to come down to dinner, at once—please.'

She's added the please as an afterthought of her own, Vicki thought involuntarily. Slight hysteria was surfacing in her. After all his innuendoes and open threats, he had now sent, like any civilised twentieth-century host, to inform her that dinner was ready. But she knew that she could not face another encounter with this particular host again tonight.

She propped herself up on one elbow and said very firmly, 'Thank you, Monique, but please tell Monsieur Laroque that I am not at all hungry and therefore I shall not be coming down to dinner.' And as the girl, round-eyed and open-mouthed, stared at her, she swung her legs off the bed and stood up. 'I'm very tired and I'm going to bed.'

When the maid had gone, she leaned against the open window, watching the sun lose itself behind the mountains, leaving them etched black, its last rays of pale gold light gilding the valley below. It was all nonsense, what he was doing, of course. She ought to laugh in his face—and yet up here among the mountains these were proud, fiercely independent people, for centuries recognising no outside authority and subdued only when the kings of France had hurled their whole might against them.

She half expected him to burst in through the door, fully intent on dragging her down to dinner, by her hair if necessary. But her bedroom door remained safely closed. Maybe he too had decided on a cessation of hostilities, at least for tonight. In any case, it appeared that she had won this particular skirmish, however minor it might be. But who would win the war?

Vicki slept late next morning. While she was showering, someone left a breakfast tray of rolls, fruit juice and coffee, and she ate slowly and deliberately, not allowing her mind to wander far from the food.

She put on one of the T-shirts that Monique had brought, and a faded blue mini denim skirt, so large that it sat, not on her waist, but across her hip-bones. Just as well, though, she thought, as she surveyed the length of slim leg, which it was revealing even so.

She picked up her tray, but as she opened the bedroom door the telephone pealed below in the hall. Vicki heard a woman's voice, which she did not recognise, and then moments later hurried footsteps and a deep voice. 'Laroque here.'

Easily overcoming her scruples at eavesdropping, Vicki strained to hear every word of the one-sided conversation. This was not difficult, for the volley of quickfire exclamations rapidly reached a crescendo and then the receiver was slammed down. There was a peremptory shout, a series of rapid commands, and then, she suddenly realised, someone was bounding up the stairs two or three at a time.

With a gasp of horror, she leapt back from the open doorway so that the china on her tray lurched perilously to one side, and pushed the door to. When, a few seconds later, there was a perfunctory knock and he came in, she was standing in the middle of the room, the peony-red flush of guilt still burning on her cheeks.

However, he did not seem to notice, or maybe it was because that he too was flushed, but with anger—no, *rage*, she thought, trying hard to study him dispassionately. His mouth was a tight line, his eyes changed to an inky blackness, his dark brows cast in a lowering scowl. But she felt instinctively that, whatever it was that had provoked this fury in him, it had nothing to do with her, and, mingled with her relief was a sense almost of smugness that, on this occasion at least, the heavens were not about to empty themselves over her.

'Victoria,' he began, without ceremony, 'I have to go out for the day. In view of your foolishness yesterday, I would prefer to take you with me,' mercifully, he did not appear to notice the violent start she gave, 'but that is not possible. However,' he paused and subjected her to a penetrating stare, 'you will, I trust, behave sensibly?'

Behind the innocuous words there was a mute, steely warning, but Vicki somehow remained totally expressionless, even as her active brain was leapfrogging ahead.

'Oh, yes, Monsieur Laroque——'

He grimaced. 'Gilles.'

'I'm sorry,' she said obediently, 'Gilles.'

'I have your word?'

'I shall be extremely sensible, I promise.' And so I shall, she told herself stoutly, even as she arranged her face into contrite humility and sugared her voice with a sweetness which nauseated her.

'Hmm.' He gazed at her speculatively for a moment, but then, as though satisfied by her submissive expression, nodded slightly to himself. 'Ask Madame Duval—my housekeeper—for anything you wish.' He turned on his heel, then said over his shoulder, 'I shall see you tonight—at dinner.'

He gave her a meaning look which said, more emphatically than words, So you will not be allowed to hide yourself away in here again, and closed the door behind him.

Vicki listened to his retreating footsteps, then moved across to the window. On the drive, the Land Rover was parked, two men in denim dungarees and sleeveless sheepskin jerkins leaning against it, smoking. As the front door opened, they hastily straightened up, tossing away their cigarettes, then climbed in beside Laroque. The doors slammed and the vehicle roared off down the drive.

Thoughtfully, she rearranged the china on her tray. He had gone for the day. Whatever this sudden emergency was, it had presented her, as neatly as if on this plate, with a twenty-four-carat opportunity. She would make another bid for freedom—she hadn't lied to him, for after all, what could be more sensible than that? And this time—her soft mouth set in a line of determination—she was going to succeed. All the same—momentarily her fingers tightened on the tray—if he was angry this morning, just how would he react when he returned and found her gone? Still, she wouldn't be here to see it . . .

In the hall there was a grey-haired woman in black—Madame Duval, presumably. She took her tray with a half-smile of approbation.

'Monsieur Laroque has gone out?' Vicki asked guilelessly.

'Yes, *mademoiselle.* He has gone across the border into Spain.'

Spain? But that was miles away. Still, so much the better.

'Can I do anything for you, *mademoiselle*?'

'Yes, please. I want to do some writing, and I've lost my notebook and pen. Could you let me have some writing materials?'

When Madame had gone, Vicki turned hastily to the huge old pictorial map of the area which she'd seen hanging in its gilt frame beside the front door. Almost trembling with suspense, she ran an unsteady finger across the glass. This must be the valley and, yes, here was the house, its gables, turrets and steep roof drawn and coloured with delicate precision. The next valley, parallel to this, like two fingers on an outspread hand, was separated from it only by a huge outcrop of mountain—the one she could see from her bedroom window.

There was obviously no hope of escape through Laroque's village; she was certain that, in spite of her air of dutiful resignation, the two young guards would already be at their posts. But behind the house—surely, he would not have thought to set his warders right up under the very shadow of the mountain. And yet, perhaps if she was lucky—*yes*. Her finger stilled and she breathed the word aloud. Here was a path, clearly marked and complete with a group of tiny figures, the women in highly unsuitable crinolines perched perilously on small donkeys. It curved round a mile or so above the house and came back almost on itself into the adjoining valley, where there was another village, and beyond that a main road, and beyond that still...

On the paved terrace at the side of the house there were some sun-loungers. She dragged one of them round into the small apple orchard behind the stable yard, then ostentatiously settled herself under the shade of a tree and set to work, recreating from memory the notes which she had casually left in the glove compartment of her hire car.

Several times, she heard footsteps—not surreptitious, just quiet—cross the yard and pause briefly, but she remained apparently thoroughly engrossed in her work. Without a watch it was difficult to be certain of the passage of time, but when she judged that at least an hour had gone she quietly screwed on the top of the fountain pen and sat waiting, every nerve-end tingling.

When once more those footsteps had come, paused and then retreated again, she put down the pen and stood up. She was surprised how apprehensive she felt now that the moment had come. She had assured

Laroque that she would be sensible, but was it really wise of her to venture up into those towering peaks with just a memorised map as her guide? Oh, what nonsense! She wasn't about to undertake a full-scale mountaineering expedition. An hour's gentle stroll through the pinewoods which she could see stretching away behind the house—and which would provide her with ideal cover—and then she would be in the next valley. This time tomorrow she could even be touching down in London, Gilles Laroque, his taunts and threats, all safely removed from the frightening present to the harmless past.

Vicki plumped down on a moss-encrusted boulder and despondently surveyed the tattered remains of the pink plastic sandals. One strap had gone early on, but she had managed a makeshift repair by twisting together several of the spiky reeds which were growing in a patch of damp ground into a strap of sorts. A few minutes before, though, she had unwarily stepped on some loose scree which had turned under her, wrenching the other strap from its flimsy moorings.

She drew her knees up to her chin and stared gloomily back the way she had come. The track, so wide and grassy when she had set out, had narrowed as it climbed, and now had all but petered out into rough flinty stones. She had missed the path. There was no point in deluding herself any longer. She knew that several hours had passed, hours when she had done nothing but climb, until her knees and calves had crumpled to jelly, her ankles to matchwood.

Beneath her lay the way she had struggled, the long curves of hills cutting her off from the valley, while above . . . when she glanced round, almost fearfully, she saw straight ahead, high above the tops of the pine trees, a line of sharp pinnacles of rock, rising as though from the shoulders of the lesser mountains which surrounded them.

'Oh, what shall I do?' She did not realise she had spoken the words aloud until she heard her own voice, high and shrill, then she started and looked about her anxiously, as though fearing that someone—or something—might also have heard her. The pines, crowding in on what remained of the track, were already dark, cast into purple shadow by the sun falling behind the highest peak. It was just the sort of place where you might see an evil, troll-like face peeping out from behind a trunk, or hear a stealthy footfall...

Somehow Vicki pushed away the agitation which was threatening to turn any minute into full-blown panic, and leapt to her feet. Surely, even if she'd missed the original path, there must be others—this area was criss-crossed with shepherds' trackways which had existed for at least a thousand years. She knew that from the work she'd been doing. Well, then, all that she had to do was to keep going and soon—by the time she'd counted to one hundred, with any luck—she would surely hit one of those elusive paths.

One, two, three... She walked on, her toes clenched to keep her sandals in place, her feet crunching on a century of decaying pine needles, their crisp, pungent scent all around her...

Four hundred... The first drop of rain fell on her face just as the track finally gave up the ghost beside a swirling torrent which tumbled across her path. On the further bank was—nothing, except for the bleak, scarred mountainside.

Above her, threatening clouds had sidled up unnoticed; below her rolled the dark pines, the soughing of their branches the only sound, apart from the rasping of her own breath. The only movement was a bird of prey, hanging in the air overhead. She shivered. Oh, please, why didn't somebody come?

Her mouth was as parched as a limekiln. Shakily, she knelt and caught up some of the water in her cupped hands, but its icy coldness burned her throat. She slowly straightened up, then—surely, yes, from far below, there was a faint sound, a soft whine. Someone must be down there—a woodsman perhaps, using a chainsaw. Until her heart leapt with joyful relief, she had not fully appreciated just how frightened she had been. Now, suddenly, she was not alone on a hostile mountain any longer.

She took a few steps back down the uneven track, then froze. Over to her right, from among the trees, burst a powerful-looking motorbike. Terrified that the rider might not see her, she waved and began stumbling across the rough scree and grass. But there was no need to worry. The rider had seen her—he'd changed direction and was now heading straight for her, skilfully using both feet as though in a cross-country scramble to guide the huge black machine swiftly up the rugged hillside.

Vicki, screwing up her eyes against the rain, gave a sudden wail of disbelief—and terror. No crash helmet...black hair...broad shoulders... It couldn't be—he was in Spain! But even while this reassuring thought echoed inanely in her brain, every fibre of common sense was urging her to flee shrieking into the mountains. On the other hand—what was that comforting old Chinese proverb? Confront a bully and he shrinks to nothing... He was near enough now for her to see his face; she turned to run.

The abrupt silence as the engine was cut dinned in her ears, then, behind her, were footsteps which themselves managed to convey the impression of intense anger. Blinded by panic, she put her foot down hard on a precarious boulder which capsized, bringing her down to her knees, then she was seized from behind and roughly hauled upright. As he took a firmer grip of her, she fought wildly, the glimpses she had of his expression only adding to her struggles. Even so, she sensed that he was using just sufficient of his strength to contain her without hurting her, but she also knew that she would not break free, and so at last she hung in his arms, fighting now only for her breath, which came in long, shuddering gasps.

'So, you are also a liar!' He shook her angrily. 'You gave me your word that you would not try to escape again.'

A grey tide of helpless weariness was enveloping her like a shroud, but his words stung her into anger in her turn.

'No, I didn't. All I promised was that I'd be sensible—and I was,' she added defiantly.

'Really?' The mocking sarcasm of his raised brows infuriated her.

'Yes—really. I was being extremely sensible. I was making for the next valley, putting as much distance between me and——'

'In that case, perhaps you'll tell me why you're heading with such purpose in entirely the wrong direction. There is no way out of this valley, unless,' he looked down meaningfully at the pathetic remnants of sandals, 'you were intending to scale those high peaks. Well?' he prompted impatiently.

'I must have misread the map in the hall,' she muttered reluctantly. 'I thought there was a path through the woods to the village in the next valley.'

'You should have asked me, and I would have advised you to consult a more helpful guide.' Still that cold sarcasm. 'That is a charming antique, but hardly the most reliable of maps. That path was completely swept away by an avalanche when I was a child.'

So it had all been a total, useless waste of time. Vicki's lips tightened. He shook his head, as though in genuine puzzlement.

'Why must you be so *entêtée*—so wilful?'

'There's no need for you to translate,' she said coldly. 'I understand perfectly well, thank you. And why must *you* be so—so unreasonable?' And stubborn, difficult, dictatorial, proud as Lucifer...

She was ransacking her mind for other terms of silent abuse, but stopped abruptly. There was an expression in his eyes—if it had not been utterly impossible, she could almost have sworn that, word for word, he knew exactly what insults she had been mentally showering on him.

'Your housekeeper said you'd gone to Spain,' she said hurriedly. 'You were back quickly.'

'Quicker than you anticipated, no doubt.' He shrugged. '*Enfin*, I did not have to cross into Spain. I caught up with them on the border.' When she looked at him in puzzlement, he went on, 'Did not Madame Duval tell you why I had gone?'

'No, and I didn't ask,' she replied, with a hint of pride.

'I went to retrieve my prize ram.'

'Your *ram*?' Vicki laughed incredulously.

His blue eyes flashed an imperious warning. 'It is not a cause for amusement, I assure you. I bought him one month ago, paying the highest price ever for a pure-bred Pyrenean ram, to improve the quality of our stock, and the thieves, who have been active in the mountains for some time now, no doubt knew exactly what they were taking. Still,' he casually examined the knuckles of his right hand, which she now saw were split right across, 'I do not think that they will be tempted to try that trick again—at least, not on me.'

'And where is he now?'

'Who? Oh, Casanova.' He looked at her darkly, as though daring her to laugh. 'That is what my shepherds have named him, out of respect for his—er—performance so far. He is safely back in the pastures, none the worse, apparently, for his ordeal. But then, when I at last got back, it was to be informed that you also had vanished. When we return, I shall have some words to say to my staff for being so negligent——'

'Oh, please, no. They were keeping a close eye on me, I promise you. It's just that——'

'—that you were too cunning for them.' Was there just a hint of reluctant respect in his tone? 'But I can assure you that they were gravely concerned for you.'

'You mean they were scared about how you would take the news. I suppose they're just as terrified of you as——' She stopped abruptly.

'You little fool.' He shook her again, his fingers biting deeply into her upper arms. 'They were concerned only that if you had wandered off into the mountains and were forced to spend the night up here, you might very well have died of exposure.'

Vicki glanced round and repressed a shudder. The dusk was setting fast, the mountains silently retreating into it. How foolhardy she'd been, and yet even a night out here alone in these uncaring peaks would surely have been preferable to——

'When I learned that you had gone, I was almost tempted to leave you to your fate.'

'But instead, of course, you came hounding after me.' Her fears—both of the night and of him—added to the waspishness in her tone. 'Otherwise, of course, you might never have been repaid, might you?'

He regarded her thoughtfully for an instant, his eyes narrowed. 'That is true. And besides, it would have been such a waste for a lovely young body to be picked clean by the bone-crushers.'

'B-bone-crushers?'

'The name the border people give to the eagle-vultures that inhabit this region. Most appropriate, don't you think? But perhaps you are right—I should not, after all, have pursued you. A thousand apologies. As you are such a lover of the mountains and so clearly wish to be alone with nature, I shall hound you no further.'

As she stared disbelievingly at him, he turned casually away. Was he really going to leave her, all alone, in the rain and the darkness? Well, all right. If that was what he wanted, she certainly wasn't going to grovel for mercy. She looked round again. Behind her, only the lighter sky showed where the jagged, broken teeth of the peaks were lost in black night. Whatever awaited her down below in the valley, she knew she could not stay here.

'No—wait, please.' She put her hand on his arm.

He stopped. 'Yes, Victoria?' It was too dark to see his face.

'I'm—sorry.' The words were dragged out of her reluctant self. 'Please, don't leave me here.'

'Come, then.' And, taking hold of her wrist, he led her across to where he had abandoned his motorbike.

He swung the huge machine upright, then gestured her to sit on the rider's seat. 'I think, on balance,' he said reflectively, 'it will be preferable for you to be in front of me, where I can see you.'

Very gingerly Vicki settled herself on the narrow, padded seat, but when she glanced down she saw that the denim skirt had ridden up to reveal her thighs. She yanked at it ineffectually, then shrugged in resignation. There was little now that could add to her humiliation, and in any case it was almost dark—he might just possibly not notice the length of leg which stretched virtually from ankle-bone to crotch.

A moment later she felt him swing his long leg easily across behind her. She stared straight ahead as he experimentally shifted his position on the pillion, but when she furtively edged herself forward he said peremptorily, 'Sit still. Now—lean back against me to balance us.'

Tentatively, she eased herself back until she came up against his hard body. He stretched past her to put his hands on the bar, his fingers brushing her bare arm.

'You're cold.'

'N-no, I'm not,' she said through chattering teeth. She couldn't possibly explain that it was not the cold that was chilling her right through.

But he put his legs on the ground to brace them, then peeled off his fleece-lined leather jacket. 'Put it on.'

She wanted to refuse, but his tone would tolerate no argument, so silently she slipped her arms into the sleeves, feeling as she did so the heat from his body, almost his very vitality, enclosing her in the warm cloth. He took hold of the bar again, one hand poised on the ignition, then paused. His breath fanned softly against her cheek, disturbing a strand of already disordered chestnut hair.

'You know, you have led me quite a dance these last two days, Victoria. But that is over now, *hein*?'

'D-do you think so?' She wanted to sound pertly defiant, but the words insisted on emerging as a husky, uncertain croak.

'Oh, yes.' She felt his right leg thrust down hard on the pedal, trapping her bare thigh between the cold metal and his own tautly muscled thigh, and the machine powered into throbbing life. 'You will not run away from me again.'

CHAPTER FOUR

'DINNER will be in one hour. You will be ready, please.'

Vicki only nodded. Still knocked out by that terrifying, exhilarating swoop down the mountainside—the brilliant shaft of headlight illuminating at one moment a sheer face of black rock, the next, a stark row of sombre pine trunks, and, above everything else, the constant awareness of his firmly braced body as the force of the wind thrust her back against him—she did not feel able to trust her voice. Besides, everything, herself included, seemed to be developing an alarming tendency to float just above the ground.

She suddenly realised that Gilles was frowning at her. 'You are very pale. Are you not well?'

'Oh, yes.' She backed up hastily against the huge oak post at the foot of the staircase. 'I—I'm fine.' She shrugged herself out of his jacket and handed it to him. 'Thank you.'

Turning, she put her foot on the first tread, then stopped dead. The green-carpeted stairs were all at once the mountainside again, stretching away into darkness, while her legs were trembling so that she must sit down... As her knees began to sag under the weight of her weightless body, Gilles caught her up into his arms.

'I asked you if you were unwell. Why do you always prevaricate? No—be quiet,' he cut her off impatiently as she tried to speak, and carried her upstairs, shouldering open her bedroom door.

He set her down carefully in the armchair beside the window where, aeons before, she had plotted the escape attempt which had taken her merely in a perfect circle back to this room. He switched on the bedside light, closed the shutters, then stood regarding her, his lips pursed.

'Would you like a cognac?'

Ugh! Just the thought of the burning liquid coursing down to her stomach made her feel queasy. 'N-no, thank you.'

He nodded. 'You are probably right. You have not, I take it, eaten all day?'

She frowned consideringly. Yes, he was right—although she hadn't been aware of it until now. Since breakfast, apart from a handful of rather tasteless whinberries which she had found by the track, she had eaten absolutely nothing. She nodded reluctantly.

'In that case, no cognac. On a completely empty stomach,' he spread his hands in an expressive gesture, 'who knows what effect alcohol might have?'

His voice was dry, but she was well aware of his meaning. In her relief at being found she had all but forgotten why, just hours previously, it had been so imperative to be safely away from this house, free from the very man who had snatched her from that hateful rainswept mountainside. Out of the frying pan, into the fire... Very fitting, she thought wryly. And this fire—would it burn, scorch, consume her in its flames...?

He squatted down on his haunches and, taking her small, chilled hand between his warm ones, began methodically massaging it, until she felt the blood flow back into it, down to her very finger-ends in a tingling, scarlet tide. When she risked a covert glance, he was totally engrossed in what he was doing; without looking up, he set down one hand and took up the other, rubbing it between his so that she felt the hard callus on his palm brush against her own tender skin.

Those hands . . . large and strong . . . sunburnt, hardworking, capable hands. And yet, at the same time, sensitive, caring . . . To have those hands, those long fingers, roam lightly, persuasively over her whole body, exploring, exploding it into a sensual heat that she had never experienced . . .

She realised that her face was burning, that her breath was coming fast and shallow, and involuntarily she moved her hand slightly. Gilles looked up, straight into her face, and for a swift, fleeting second their eyes caught and held. Something flared between them, then, as quickly as a match-flame struck in the dark, died.

'I'm quite warm now. Thank you.'

She drew her hands back and, not looking at him, smoothed her brief skirt down unsteadily. With an effort at normality, she said, 'Is that how you treat your lambs—when they're sick, I mean?'

He sat back on his haunches, his eyes on her fingers, which were picking nervously at the raised seam of her skirt. 'On occasion.'

'So you don't leave it all to your shepherds?'

Her voice still had that light quality, as though she couldn't get her breath easily. Oh, why didn't he stand up? His knee was carelessly brushing against her leg, the cloth of his jeans strained against his inner thigh. He was doing—absolutely nothing—and yet she felt a scarcely perceptible yet still palpable threat emanating from him.

As she moved restlessly in the chair, he suddenly straightened up. 'Oh, no. Not that all my shepherds are not excellent, but I prefer to keep charge myself. And besides,' his voice took on a lazy, sensuous quality, 'lambs are such attractive, helpless, endearing little creatures that I find them——' without warning, he bent over her and lifted her, unprotestingly, to her feet '—perfectly irresistible.'

He held her from him at arm's length as though to study her reaction to his words, and Vicki felt herself colour hotly. Her eyelashes flickered and fell to the brown V of chest, her eyes feverishly chasing round and round the small, gold St Christopher medallion which encircled his strong throat.

'Well, at least you are less pale now.' Surely there was the faintest undercurrent of irony?

She pulled away from him. 'I—I must get ready for dinner,' she said unsteadily.

'But of course.' His voice, she noted resentfully, was perfectly controlled. 'Come down as soon as you are ready.'

Vicki longed for nothing more than to soak every tired, aching limb in a long, luxurious bath, but she did not dare delay, so instead settled for a quick shower. She pulled a perfunctory comb through her bedraggled hair, then tied it back into a soft ponytail. From the wardrobe she pulled out a simple cotton dress in a dark Provençal print and slipped into it, feeling that twinge of sadness which she experienced each time she put on these borrowed clothes. That poor young woman, Monique's sister... Scalding tears pricked at her eyes. Such tragedy, such unhappiness everywhere... A gong sounded in the hall. She turned, and almost ran out of the room.

Half-way down the staircase, though, she froze into stillness. Gilles was below her, leaning against one of the ornate antique gilt side tables, his arms crossed, frowning at the carpet as though at some imponderable problem. He too had showered; his hair was still curling damply into his neck, and he had changed into narrow-legged black trousers and a silky-knit polo shirt.

Dressed all in black, his dark brows drawn down in that frown, he seemed all at once very intimidating again. She hovered uncertainly, all her instincts now urging her to turn and flee back to the sanctuary of her room. But that would be futile. Tonight he would undoubtedly come up and fetch her. Even as she hesitated, he glanced up and saw her; she expelled one deep, long-held breath and went on down.

The dining-room, panelled in pale, honey-gold oak and carpeted in a deeper gold, glowed softly under the light from the silk-shaded wall-lamps. At one end of the long expanse of polished table, a pair of ornate candlesticks, their silver turned by many years of loving care from sharp brilliance to a soft, almost misty patina, cast a tiny oasis of light in which two places had been set.

A cosy tête-à-tête dinner for two? No, far more likely, Vicki thought, as she surveyed the small circle of gleaming glasses, cutlery and china, that he wanted to keep a very close eye on her. After all, regarding her as he did as some kind of investment, perhaps he intended, like the witch in *Hansel and Gretel*, to fatten her up. The witch, though, had only planned to eat her captive, whereas... That same emotion which had so paralysingly gripped her on the staircase swept through her again.

Gilles pulled back a chair for her, and she sank down into it, her legs trembling, just as Monique, in a neat black dress and white apron, appeared with a tureen of fresh vegetable soup. Vicki, her eyes on her soup bowl, had to force the first few mouthfuls down, but then she gradually felt life flowing back into her. Yes, this was all that had been wrong with her, after all—she hadn't realised until now just how ravenous she was.

She finished spooning up the soup, then wiped her mouth on the linen napkin.

'Would you like some more?'

She looked up, to see Gilles, on the far side of the small pool of light, watching her, the faintest smile lurking at the corner of his lips.

'Oh, no.' Without being aware of it, she had, she now realised, been scraping assiduously at her bowl, taking up every last morsel, so that the delicate pattern on the old Meissen dish was in grave danger of being wiped clean. She flushed with embarrassment and added stiltedly, 'It was delicious, but no more, thank you.'

She sat in silence as Monique brought in silver dishes of vegetables, plates whose pattern matched that on the soup bowls, and finally an enormous oval dish with a leg of roast lamb, its sizzling brown skin spiked with the fragrance of rosemary sprigs. Gilles pushed back his chair and, picking up the huge carving knife, began deftly cutting wafer-thin slices of meat, as the maid held a plate for him.

He looked at Vicki enquiringly. 'Is that sufficient—at least, to begin with?'

She shook her head. 'None for me, thank you.'

Tapping the knife impatiently against the serving plate, he scowled at her. 'What *bêtise* is this? I have told you, you must eat.'

'I don't want any meat,' Vicki said levelly. 'I'm a vegetarian.'

He stared at her with rather the same expression, she thought, as though she had just said, 'I'm a Martian,' but he merely repeated, 'A vegetarian?'

'Yes.' The incredulity in his voice needled her and she added, 'You do have them in France, don't you?'

'I believe so—although it has never, until now, been my privilege to meet one.'

He was still tapping the knife softly against the plate, and for a moment she thought that he intended tying her into her chair and force-feeding her, but then he took the plate from Monique and said something in dialect to her. When the girl had gone out, he remarked, 'I take it that you do not object to an omelette? It is rather short notice for my cook to produce anything more elaborate.'

'Yes, thank you. I'm sorry—I should have told you earlier, but that will be very nice.'

He set the well-filled plate down in his own place. 'I trust you will not object if I do not abstain? Although I do not keep my sheep for their meat, it would be anathema to any self-respecting livestock farmer to indulge in vegetarianism.'

Indulge was not the word she would have chosen, but instead she only said evenly, 'What do you keep them for, then?'

He helped himself from a dish of sliced *haricots verts*. 'At the moment, only their fleeces—we produce some of the famous Pyrenean wool. You have perhaps heard of it?'

'Yes.' She paused, then added, 'I've got a dressing-gown made from it. It's beautifully warm.'

David had bought it for her, to help her withstand the arctic temperatures of their elegant, high-ceilinged draughty old fridge of a house in London. That had been their last Christmas together... Oh, what a mess everything was. Now, her home was a small, neat, centrally heated box in a modern block of boxes. Suddenly, overpoweringly, she ached with the desperation to be safely back there, surrounded by the security of all her possessions...

Monique set before her a large omelette, overflowing with tiny sautéd mushrooms, and blindly she began to eat, just as Gilles, leaning across to fill her glass with wine, asked casually, 'Tell me, who is David?'

Vicki started so violently that her fork rattled against the plate. Was he telepathic? Her eyes flew to him, but he was seemingly engrossed in filling his own glass.

'D-David?' she prevaricated, then, flatly, 'How do you know about him?'

He set down the bottle. 'While you were drugged, you lay most of the time in a stupor, but then you would rouse and begin to talk wildly to this David.'

'W-what did I say?' She was holding her voice together with extreme care.

'Oh—very little that was coherent.' He paused briefly. 'Well, who is he—this David who appears to occupy such a large part of your mind?'

There was a short silence. She wanted to tell him that it was none of his business, but there was a tautness in his voice which somehow warned her that such a response would be futile.

'My husband.'

'Your—husband?'

Well, if she'd been setting out to create an effect, she couldn't have been more successful. He stared across the table at her, blank astonishment vivid in his eyes and, just for a moment, something else as well.

'My ex-husband, I should have said. I'm——' the words were being torn from her '—divorced.'

He surveyed her judicially. 'So.' He nodded, as though assimilating this information. 'But you did not leave him, I think? I see the pain in your eyes, therefore he left you.'

Her lips twisted. 'You could say that.'

'He had met someone else?'

Vicki moved restlessly in her chair. She didn't have to put up with this inquisition. He had no right to question her, to tear from her these facts which were still so wounding for her. And yet, might it not be a relief to tell—not everything, of course—the pain was too raw, her own pitifully ravaged pride too vulnerable still—but at least some of it? The misery, the shame had festered untold in her for so long, unable as she'd been to accept the sympathy that had been held out to her, but here maybe she might gain something of the relief to be found in the Confessional, in unburdening herself to this hard, impersonal man who would soon, once again, be a stranger to her. Telling him might offer a sort of peace, a sort of catharsis.

'Yes,' she said at last. 'He found—someone else.'

'This David,' he sounded almost angry, 'he must be very foolish, to look elsewhere. You are, of course, far too thin, but otherwise you are not——' he gave her a smile which was faintly wry '—unattractive. He must have found someone very special indeed.'

'Yes, you could say that.' Vicki clamped her lips together as her eyes brimmed with tears under his searching gaze.

'Forgive me, Victoria, if this is hurtful for you.' His voice had softened perceptibly. 'We will say no more.'

'No, it's all right. I—I met him in my first year at the college where I was doing a media studies course. He was one of the lecturers.' She frowned slightly. 'I suppose at first I was just flattered—he was so handsome, so much older than me—but then I really fell for him. We were married in my final year.' Her voice was weary, swept clean of any emotion.

'And how long did the marriage last?'

'Less than two years. We were divorced just over a year ago.'

'So this explains the hurt that hovers perpetually in your eyes, like that of some wounded creature. And yet——' he seemed now to be speaking to himself '—you have still a strangely innocent, *untouched* air.' She stirred restlessly again as he went on, 'And you are how old now?'

'Twenty-four.'

He nodded again, more decisively this time, as though now consigning her marriage to oblivion. 'But you are young enough, *ma petite*, to put all this behind you, to begin again.' Would that it were so simple, she thought. 'Believe me, Victoria, it is true. The older one becomes, the more difficult it also becomes when one is badly hurt to—what do you say?—wipe the slate clean, and begin life again.' There was a harsh edge to his voice now which penetrated her unhappiness, and when she glanced up she saw for an instant naked anger—and yes, pain, in his own eyes.

Their gaze held for a moment, but then, as Monique returned and began clearing away the plates and dishes, he said briskly, 'This media studies course—what is that?'

Grateful to be on more neutral ground, Vicki replied, 'Well, it's to do with communications. You know, radio, TV, advertising, that sort of thing. When I left college I worked for a time as a copywriter in an advertising agency.'

She was speaking more freely now but, looking across at him, she broke off as she saw with surprise that he was eyeing her in what could only be described as a speculative manner.

'And what do you do now?'

'I freelance, mainly for a small, independent film-making company, as a researcher and writer.'

'Freelance? I do not understand. Do they employ you?'

'They did. But then,' she clasped her hands tightly in her lap, 'I was—ill, for several months last year, so—they replaced me. I came here to research a programme idea I had, about Montaillou—that village which in the thirteenth century was the centre of the Cathar heresy——'

'Yes, yes, I know—it is a fascinating story.'

'I was planning to build it around the *châtelaine*, Béatrice de Planissoles, who got herself involved with the village priest.'

'Among others.' His voice was dry. 'Yes, the Lady Béatrice must have been quite a girl.'

'But it doesn't seem to be working out—not as a TV programme, anyway, which is what I was hoping for.'

Her voice tailed away. While she was ill, she had read the fascinating account of the everyday, intimate doings of the medieval villagers, so like those of ordinary people the world over today—the bickerings, the friendships, the loves—and the hates—and had seen in it her way back to a normal life. But now, when eventually she returned to London, it would be with the inescapable knowledge that she would have nothing to offer.

As Monique served the pudding, Vicki sat lost in her own unhappy thoughts, but when she saw the darkly rich chocolate soufflé topped with burnt almonds and the dish of whipped cream she could not resist a smile of pleasure.

'Stage two of your fattening-up process?' Her smile widened to an impish grin, but he merely gave her an enigmatic look in return.

'Oh, I assure you, Victoria, I seldom interfere in domestic matters—you must blame my cook for any such scheme.'

When they had finished, he led the way into the adjoining sitting-room. It was extremely spacious and obviously very old, but someone had renovated it with great care and love. The creamy stone walls had been exposed, and a huge stone fireplace reached as far as the ancient, beamed ceiling. In spite of its size, though, the room was far from forbidding. Although it was only September, a cosy log fire crackled on the enormous open hearth, and a sofa and several armchairs in moss-green velvet were drawn up around it.

A beautiful Persian rug lay in front of the hearth, and a low table stood on it, complete with a tray of coffee.

'What a lovely room!' Vicki exclaimed, as she sank into one of the armchairs.

'Yes, my parents renovated it when they were first married. It is an old tradition in our family that each generation adds something to the house. My grandfather and great-grandfather were responsible for building on the new wing—you have perhaps noticed that the house is in a variety of styles. This room is part of the very oldest section, the fifteenth-century core of the house.'

'Goodness,' said Vicki faintly. 'And you—what have you done?'

'Black or white coffee?'

'Oh, white, please.'

He added some cream, then handed her the cup. 'I have done nothing,' he said briefly. 'You would like a liqueur?'

He filled two glasses and set one beside her. She picked it up and held it to the light, so that the liquid glowed soft emerald, then sipped it tentatively. 'Mmm, it's delicious.' She felt it slide like warm silk down her throat. 'What is it?'

'Izarra. It is distilled from flowers and herbs which grow high in the Pyrenees.'

He drained his coffee-cup and sat for some moments, drumming his fingers on the arm of his chair. Then he stood up abruptly.

'I would like to fetch something for you to see.'

As she looked up at him, wide-eyed, he crossed rapidly to the door. He opened it, then paused. 'Wait here.'

The meaning was quite clear, but Vicki, lulled by the warmth of the fire and the liqueur was, in any case, in no state to attempt yet another flight. She yawned hugely and leaned back in her chair, running her finger idly round and round the rim of her cup. She gazed meditatively at it, wondering what it was that he was bringing to show her, then realised with a start that the band around the pretty pink and white Limoges cup was nothing less than pure silver.

She was just replacing the cup, with extreme care, when Gilles returned. He was carrying a large blue leather folder, which he handed to her.

'I would like your opinion—your professional opinion—of this.'

Wonderingly, she opened it and drew out several sheets of card, with colour photographs and pieces of writing, in English, pasted on them. It was clearly a mock-up of some sort of publicity brochure for—she saw as she looked more closely—a range of sheep's milk products—yogurts, soft cheeses blended with herbs and garlic, and so on. She spread the items out on the hearth-rug and knelt over them.

'Well, what do you think?' His voice had a hint of impatience, but she was still skimming through the papers. One of the illustrations was of the pastures, the mountains behind and in the foreground a group of alert-looking sheep knee deep in buttercups. Another was of the house, with Gilles leaning against a superb peacock-blue Renault Alpine sports car. Someone, she saw, had actually managed to lure him into a jacket and tie. As she examined the photograph, for the first time the full realisation flooded through her of just how astonishingly handsome he was... She hastily tore her eyes back to the innocuous phrases: '...a wholly new taste concept...'

'Hmm.' She glanced up. 'The pictures are fine—although I think maybe,' she hesitated, then went on, 'this one of you—I think you'd be better in working clothes. You look a bit too—well, formal—as though you wouldn't really know one end of a sheep from the other.'

He laughed. 'Yes, perhaps you are right. And the rest?'

'Well, the layout's all right on the whole, but the real problem is the copy.'

'Copy?'

'The words. I presume this is intended for English readers?'

'Yes. Until now, our export business has been solely in wool and wool products, but I wish to diversify. I intend to enter the exclusive foods market in England—I plan to arrange contracts with some of your major stores—and then, when this is established, move into North America.'

'Well, in that case, the English isn't quite right. It reads a bit like one of those manuals for a Far-East computer—you know, it's almost too literal. Here, for instance—"formidable". You can't really talk about formidable cheeses—it sounds as if they'd keep you awake all night with indigestion.' Even as she smiled up at him, a horrifying thought struck her. 'You didn't write it, did you?'

'No, but it is as I feared.' He spoke reflectively, but Vicki saw a spark of anger in those dark blue eyes. 'It is not satisfactory.'

'I'm sorry,' Vicki pulled a rueful face, 'But you did ask me. If I were doing it——'

She broke off abruptly as she realised that he had left his chair and was dropping down casually to kneel beside her and start gathering up the sheets.

'Yes?' he prompted. 'If you were doing it?'

'Well, I——' Her voice was suddenly husky. He was very near her. She could smell the mingled tang of the outdoors, spicy aftershave and warm male body winding itself around her. If she stretched out her hand just a few inches she could touch him... She cleared her throat. 'If I were doing it, I'd start from scratch—from the beginning,' she added hastily, as he looked enquiringly at her. 'For example, the copy is presumably a translation from your French material. Well, I wouldn't just translate—I'd want to see round your enterprise, decide for myself what should be highlighted. I don't know much about dairy products, but I've got the feeling that this doesn't really do you justice.'

'And how long would such a task take, would you imagine?' His tone was perfectly non-committal.

'Oh, not too long.' She pondered, her lips pursed in mental calculation. 'It shouldn't take anyone more than a couple of weeks, I should think.'

'Hmm.' He sat back on his haunches, then, with a sudden decisive movement, snatched up the remaining sheets of typescript, ripped them across and hurled them into the heart of the crackling fire.

As Vicki gaped in horrified fascination, the papers curled, smouldered and burst into flame. 'But it wasn't that bad!' she wailed.

He shrugged. 'As you yourself said, it was not good enough.'

'But whatever will you do now?'

He looked at her consideringly for a moment, then seemed to come to a swift decision. '*Bien.* We have the answer at hand—*you* will do it for me. You will prepare another brochure. I will give you every facility, and when you have completed it, we shall consider your debt to have been fully repaid.'

CHAPTER FIVE

'BUT I thought——' Vicki blurted out, then stopped dead, the tell-tale colour flaring in her cheeks.

'Yes, Victoria?' Gilles raised his dark brows questioningly. 'You thought——?' he prompted invitingly, but she only shook her bent head.

'Oh, nothing,' she mumbled, so he completed the sentence for her.

'You thought that I intended you would pay your debt—with interest—in my bed.'

She started violently, but before she could utter the vehement denials which were already forming on her lips he went on, 'And if I am honest with you—there is, after all, no need for any pretence between us any more—that is precisely what I *had* intended.' He paused, raked her with a disconcertingly searching look, then smiled wryly. 'But, on cool reflection, it is perhaps wiser—for both our sakes—that your debt should be redeemed in this way, and that our relationship should remain on a strictly formal basis.'

So her worst fears, at least, were not to be realised. The nightmare which had haunted her since he had first hijacked her from the *auberge* and brought her here was not, after all, to be made a reality. As the relief flooded through her, she scrambled to her feet, carefully avoiding a meeting with those penetrating blue eyes, and sat primly back in the armchair, her hands folded in her lap, the primness masking her inner, dancing jubilation.

Gilles took the brass poker and prodded the logs so that the last wispy remnants of paper floated away up the wide chimney in an effervescence of sparks. Then he sprawled back in the chair opposite her, watching her thoughtfully over the arch of his fingers.

'Well?' he said at last, a shade impatiently. 'You will do it?'

Vicki hesitated. He would, she had no doubt, be a hard taskmaster, so difficult—no, impossible to please, and besides, she had done no copywriting for nearly two years. The relief which she had been hugging to herself sagged dismally all at once. She ran her tongue around her lips.

'I—I don't know,' she hedged. She should have kept her mouth firmly shut—she would never be able to produce a better brochure than the one he had just fed to the flames. And then, what would he—or rather, what wouldn't he do?

As her mind hunted frantically around for some alternative, she suddenly glimpsed a straw and grasped at it. 'You can't possibly want to entrust me with it,' she said flatly. 'After all, I'm nothing but a worthless junkie.'

'Oh, no,' he shook his head firmly. 'You are not a junkie.' He paused, then added, 'In this respect, at least, I have misjudged you.'

And that, she thought with a wry twist, was the nearest thing on earth to an abject, grovelling apology that she would ever receive from Gilles Laroque.

'And besides,' he went on unhurriedly, 'when I summoned the doctor to you——'

'Doctor?' She gaped at him blankly.

'Yes—while you were unconscious, in that disturbingly heavy sleep. He gave it as his opinion, after a thorough examination, that although you were clearly under the influence of a large quantity of some drug or other, you were not an addict,' he ignored her gasp of angry astonishment, 'and that the drug could well have been administered without your knowledge.'

Outraged, Vicki could only stare at him. At last, after an endless silence, she said, her voice shaking slightly, 'You knew! On that first morning, you knew! But y-you didn't tell me.' Her chest heaved stormily. 'Why? Why didn't you?'

He shrugged carelessly, as though the whole affair was of trifling importance. 'Because I did not choose to,' he said coolly. 'And besides, your—elusiveness over the last two days has given me little opportunity, even if I had so wished.'

Vicki smacked her hands down on the velvet arms of her chair. She desperately wanted to hurl herself across the rug, kicking him, punching that arrogant, self-contained face, yet behind all the anger some powerful instinct for self-preservation wisely held her in check. So instead, she leapt to her feet and stood, leaning an elbow on the stone mantelpiece, her fingers tapping out an angry rhythm. Conscious that he was watching her, her eyes brimmed with facile tears of frustration and she turned her head away.

She had not noticed the picture before. It hung just above the level of the mantel, very small in its gilt frame, inconspicuous from a distance, though now, from close up, it glowed softly like a jewel. The background was of brilliant orange, filled in with tiny stylised flowers and animals, while in the foreground, in front of a row of tiny orange-trees, was a small round jade and gold tent. In the doorway a young girl in a white, gold-embroidered dress sat on clumps of tiny starry daisies, one hand resting on the pure white unicorn which was just laying its head down in her lap, its horn lowered in submission to her perfect, fragile beauty.

'It is very beautiful, *n'est-ce pas*?'

Vicki started slightly, then willed herself not to turn round, or to leap away to a safe distance, as Gilles' voice came, not from the far side of thc rug, but just at her ear, his breath warm against her neck, stirring the little individual hairs.

'Yes, it is.'

To cover her prickling nervousness, she stared at it even more closely, then saw that the edges of the picture were worn, as if from long use.

'It is an illustration from a Book of Hours which was given to an ancestor of mine by one of the Dukes of Burgundy in the fourteenth century—a reward for fighting bravely against the hordes of marauding English.' His voice had taken on a faintly dry note. 'But the rest of the book has long since disappeared.'

'But surely it's very valuable?'

'Priceless,' he replied simply. 'My parents kept it for forty years in a bank strong-room, but when my father died and *Maman* moved to the Côte d'Azur, I could not bear that anything of such matchless beauty should languish in a dark vault beneath the streets of Toulouse, so I fetched it back.'

'Oh, I'm glad you did,' she said spontaneously. 'You're right—it's much too beautiful to be hidden away. But aren't you afraid it might be stolen?'

'The house is well-protected and, as those sheep thieves discovered today, it does not pay to try such tricks on me.' He smiled reminiscently, then went on casually, 'Of course, it was extremely unsuitable material for a book of prayers. A historian friend of mine thinks that this is how it has survived; it was probably ripped from the book at some time in an excess of zealous piety.'

Vicki frowned at the tiny picture in bewilderment. 'But why? How could anyone possibly be offended by it?'

Gilles laughed. 'Oh, not by the painting itself, but the meaning behind it, Victoria.' She looked up at him, puzzled, not so much by his words as by a faint something in his voice. 'The legend of the unicorn told that its horn was such a powerful aphrodisiac that men hunted it endlessly. But in spite of its beauty, it was such a fearsome creature that the only person whom it would not harm was an untouched virgin. Entranced by her purity, the unicorn would lay its head down in her lap, and only then could the hunters safely seize it.'

He paused, and Vicki stirred restlessly beneath his now almost hypnotic gaze. 'Of course, you understand the symbolism behind the myth—that in capturing the creature in this way, the young woman sacrificed to him her virginity, deflowered by the potency of his love-arousing power.'

He broke off again and Vicki, picking nervously at the stone bevelling, was conscious that he was regarding her thoughtfully. 'A strange legend, *n'est-ce pas*? But, even stranger is that you remind me very strongly of the young girl in the painting.' He put the back of his hand under her chin and gently, though irresistibly, turned her head towards him, her eyes flickering then falling before his.

'Your hair is not gold, of course, but the perfect oval shape of your face is the same, the beautifully moulded mouth,' his thumb brushed gently across her lower lip, 'delicate, though with a subtle hint of the sensuality to come. But above all, the same remote, untouched quality which I recognised in you, and which continues to intrigue me, I admit, now that I know you are not the young unmarried——'

Vicki wrenched her head back abruptly, breaking his grip—and the spell which his softly spoken words were weaving insidiously about her. She retreated to the relative safety of her armchair and stood leaning up against its back, using it to steady the trembling of her legs. As he watched her, arms folded, his face cast into shadow, he was all at once the same intimidating stranger she had seen below her in the hall, and the same spiralling panic rose again unbidden to meet her thought.

She had to get away from here. She could not escape, he had shown her that all too clearly. But he had, after all, offered her a way out. One small piece of work—work which a year ago she would have taken easily in her competent stride—and she would be free to go. He'd promised her that.

As though reading her thoughts, he said softly, 'But you still have not answered my question, Victoria.'

'Yes,' she replied rather huskily, then again, more strongly, 'Yes, I will prepare your brochure for you—to the best of my ability, that is. But I must warn you, I haven't done——'

He shook his head at her, with a faint smile. 'I think you are perhaps lacking in confidence in your talents. As for myself, I have no doubt that the result will—satisfy us both.'

He straightened up, came over to her and held out a large, tanned hand. 'We have a bargain, then, Mademoiselle Victoria Summers.'

She hesitated momentarily, then put her own small hand in his and nodded. 'A bargain, Monsieur Gilles Laroque.'

As she made to withdraw her hand, though, his grip tightened and he brought his other hand up, to close on her wrist so that she was trapped. He raised her hand, turned it over, and began very softly kissing the palm. His warm lips were doing no more than brushing the tender skin, across the palm and down each finger, and yet Vicki felt herself begin to tremble—very gently at first, then increasingly, until she felt the tremors run across from her finger-ends into his.

'Let me go!'

She dragged herself free from his grasp and he straightened up, a small, secret smile hovering fleetingly around his lips, as though she had just told him something he wanted very badly to know.

'Don't do that—ever again,' she said, rather too loudly and belligerently.

Completely unabashed, he retorted, 'Oh, but *ma chère* Victoria, you quite misunderstand me. That is only the way in which here, in the valley, we seal a bargain.' His expression was perfectly bland, but she was quite certain that secret amusement was dancing wickedly behind those dark blue eyes. 'Surely you must admit that it is much more *agréable* than a cold handshake? And now, sit down and let us have some more coffee.'

He gestured her back to her chair, but she shook her head vehemently, her chestnut hair swinging. She could not stay in this room a moment longer. His disturbing presence was making every nerve ending crackle almost audibly.

'No, I—I want to begin work right away.'

He frowned. 'Nonsense! You do not have to impress me with such industry. You are tired this evening—you will begin work in the morning. Sit down.'

'No,' she said stubbornly. 'I'm not tired now, not in the slightest.' It was not at all true, but she knew she would not sleep, not tonight. 'After all,' she added, with a hint of acid, 'the sooner I start, the sooner I finish.'

His slight frown deepened to the scowl of a man totally unused to being defied, but she tilted her chin in defiance and returned his gaze unflinchingly. The conflict of wills for at least temporary supremacy hung, almost visible, in the air between them, then he lifted one shoulder in a careless shrug.

'You are determined to make a martyr of yourself. Very well, come with me.'

Gilles' study was a small, cosy room lined with ceiling-high shelves which were crammed with books and papers. In one corner stood a large, intimidating-looking computer, while in the middle of the room was an enormous leather-topped table and swivel chair. Extremely brisk and businesslike now, he gestured her to the chair; then, as she perched on the edge, watching him, he began sorting out papers, his lips pursed in concentration. Finally, he placed a sheaf in front of her, leaned across and switched on the powerful articulated metal reading-lamp.

'These,' he tapped the papers with a long brown finger, 'will tell you something about the estate—the various enterprises and so on. Tomorrow, I shall show you around, so you will have more information then.'

He walked across to the fireplace, knelt on the huge sheepskin rug which lay in front of the hearth, switched on the gas fire, then straightened up and looked at her enquiringly. 'You have everything you need? There are pens, pencils, paper for you to use.'

Vicki, beginning to feel more secure already, smiled briefly at him from behind the expanse of table. 'Yes, thank you.'

He nodded. 'Very well. *A bientôt*, Victoria.'

'Goodnight,' she replied, and breathed a silent sigh of relief as behind her she heard the door close softly.

She picked up the first sheet of typewritten paper and tried to settle herself comfortably in the huge swivel chair. But the chair, having been designed specially—or so she suspected—to accommodate a large, bulky frame, was definitely not suited to her small, slight one.

So in the end, she gathered up all the papers, set the lamp on the floor by the fire, kicked off the remnants of sandals, took up her favourite working position, sprawled on her stomach, her chin cupped in one hand, and set to work once more on the first paper. The gas fire hissed pleasantly... the depths of the sheepskin enfolded her in sensuous warmth...

There was the touch of a large hand on her shoulder. Vicki heard herself murmuring something unintelligible, stirred, then came to with a jolt. Her eyes opened and, beyond the untidy heap of papers, she saw a pair of black-clad legs. Oh, lord, she'd fallen asleep. She'd just laid her head down for a moment after struggling with the complexities of the finer points of specialist, upmarket cheese-making, and the fire and the soft sheepskin had done the rest. She struggled to a sitting position, pushing the tangle of chestnut hair out of her eyes.

'I wasn't asleep,' she said, squinting into the merciless beam of the lamp. 'I—I was thinking—hard.'

She heard a sound which just might have been a smothered laugh, then Gilles flicked off the light, leaving only the softer blue flames of the fire.

'But of course,' he murmured in her ear. 'And also, of course, you always resemble a small, woolly, rather sleepy owl when you are thinking hard.'

Furious with herself, she sat back on her heels, snatching at her hair to tuck it behind her ears.

'What's the time?' She avoided his eyes, as he squatted on the rug beside her.

'After midnight—'

'Good heavens! How time flies when you get really caught up in your work,' she said, at the same time half suppressing a huge, jaw-breaking yawn.

'—and as I shall expect you to be up very early in the morning,' Vicki somehow smothered a despondent groan, 'I came in to insist that you go to bed now. After all, you have had a trying day, having spent most of it scaling the Pyrenees single-handed.'

He was laughing at her again. When she glanced directly at him there was no mistaking the glint of amusement in those normally cold dark blue eyes. Remembering her futile attempts to escape, her weariness—and fear, among those hostile mountain peaks, she felt a tiny flicker of anger. He was so strong, so entirely sure of himself.

Her lips tightened, but when she looked at him again the anger shrivelled suddenly into unease. The glinting amusement had vanished, to be replaced by another, much less frivolous emotion. For a fraction of a second they stared directly into each other's eyes, then, even as Vicki, frightened, began to scramble away from him and on to her feet, he reached out for her, pulled her to him, and his arms were holding her imprisoned against him.

Too shaken for a moment to speak, she could only be quite still, her hands splayed against his chest, feeling beneath the warmth of his body the strong but not quite steady beat of his heart. Her own pulses were fluttering madly—the result, no doubt, of her sudden movement a moment before, and the reason her mouth was so dry, her breathing so erratic.

Gilles' back was directly to the fire, and in the semi-darkness his expression was quite unreadable now, but she felt the tension flickering between them, coiling itself around them, until everything beyond her thumping heart and the feel of his arms tight around her had ceased to exist.

Then, very softly, he lowered his head and his lips took hers. The kiss at first was undemanding, even gentle, but then, as his arms tightened even more, she felt herself give a shuddering sigh which seemed to rack her whole body. Almost without knowing it, her lips opened, warm and welcoming, under his, and in immediate response his kiss hardened, his tongue thrusting into the softness of her mouth in intoxicating sweetness and power.

Slowly, inexorably, Gilles was bending her to his will, laying her unresistingly down on the warm depths of the sheepskin as though on a bed. She closed her eyes as the blood, a dark, heavy tide, roared in her ears; and another tide was rising in her, a surging wave of desire which, if she would only surrender to it, would sweep her away to—to what?

Her eyes flew open as, simultaneously, her head jerked back. 'Let me go!'

There was crackling panic in her voice and she punched at him, almost frantic. But for a few seconds his grip only tightened on her the more before, his eyes black in the dim light and still fixed on hers, he loosed his hands in a gesture of release and she rolled away into a tangle of crumpled papers, her chest heaving as she fought to control her breath.

'Y-you said it wouldn't be this way. You promised,' her voice trembled uncontrollably, 'that I'd p-pay you back—with this.' She gestured to the tangle of papers lying around them. 'You said it would be the w-wisest way.'

He leaned on his elbow and shot her a faintly rueful smile. 'But, *chérie*, you must know that it is not always possible to be—wise.' She realised that, despite his apparent self-control, his voice was not entirely steady. 'And after all, Victoria, we are adults, you and I. You are not a child.' His voice was quite smooth now. 'Indeed, you have been married.'

Vicki clenched her hands until the nails bit deep into the palms, but he did not miss the tiny action, even if, as his next words showed, he failed to understand its full import.

'Sexual chemistry between a man and a woman is as old as time. *You* may choose to repel it,' she winced at the sudden hardness in his tone, 'but you cannot deny its existence. You know very well that I am deeply attracted to you, and you——'

She put her hands over her ears. 'Stop it! I—I won't hear any more.' She went to stand up, but he caught her by the arm and swung her round to face him.

'And you,' he continued implacably, 'are equally attracted to me. Oh, yes, you may deny it, but your body speaks for you, Victoria—and it betrays you every time I come near you, every time I touch you.'

He lifted a hand and in the lightest, most sensuous of finger-kisses slid it across her lips, then down the line of her throat, then lower still, until for the first time he brushed directly against the high swell of her breast, so that, beneath the thin cotton of her dress, they both felt its centre tauten against the persuasive touch of his palm. Vicki bit her lip, but none the less a tiny sob escaped her, even as he lifted his hand away.

'Every time I touch you,' he was going on remorselessly, 'your body tells me——'

She had to break free, before something terrible happened. 'No, it's not true. You—you smug, *arrogant*——'

She broke his grip and stumbled to her feet, glaring defiantly down at him. He shook his head, as though a little sadly, but there was a flicker of colour along his tanned cheekbones and, strangely, the knowledge that she had angered him gave her courage. So he had expected her to slip unprotestingly, mild as one of his lambs, into his bed, as no doubt most women would have done by now. Well, he would just have to learn, once and for all, that she was not one of those women. They had shaken hands on an agreement and she was not going to have the terms of their bargain altered, merely to suit his changing mood.

'Whatever you may imagine you know about me,' she said coldly, 'the reality, for you, is simply this.

Because—quite unjustly—you refuse to release me, I have no option other than to do this work for you. But that is all—*all* that I shall do for you.'

He slowly uncoiled himself to stand by her, all but intimidating her by the sheer bulk of his frame, but she took a deep breath, which steadied her sufficiently to go on. 'I shall do the copy, as I promised, to the best of my ability, and then you will release me. Anything else would be a—complication which I am simply not prepared to accept. And so——'

He took a step towards her, his body entirely blotting out the light, and she almost trembled at the threat so clearly emanating from him, but by a supreme effort she stood her ground, willing herself to go on. 'And so, if you are not prepared to accept my conditions, well—you have forfeited all claim to keep me here.'

She turned away, desperate now to be out of the room, but a hand detained her. 'You must not be afraid of me—or of yourself, Victoria.' His voice was gentle now, and there was an understanding, almost a compassion in it which momentarily brought burning tears to her averted eyes.

'Afraid of *myself*? You must be crazy.'

'No, *ma petite*, you are afraid. For some reason, which I do not as yet understand, but which I trust in time I shall comprehend,' she stiffened in apprehension at the self-assurance of his words, 'you are almost more frightened of yourself than of anything that you think I may do. But to allay your fears of me, at least, I promise you that I shall do nothing that you do not wish, nothing that you do not welcome or seek from me.'

His hold tightened on her as she moved involuntarily and his voice took on a silky, purring quality, like that of a giant cat. 'But I also promise you that, in time, you *will* wish it, *will* welcome it.'

His words, husky with sensual promise, were weaving that seductive spell round her once more, so that her breath sang terrifyingly in her ears. With one final, desperate effort, she wrenched her arm away from his grip.

'Never!'

Her voice echoed shrilly around the room as, her feet crunching almost unheeded through the papers littered about them, she ran across to the door. She fumbled at the handle, her sweaty fingers barely able to grasp it, flung it open, then turned back to him.

'Never. Do you hear me? *Never!*'

She was trembling so much that she could hardly form the words. Gilles stood regarding her, an odd, almost tender smile on his face, which infuriated her even more. Then he nodded.

'I hear you, Victoria.'

As she banged the door to, he remained motionless, the smile still hovering on his lips.

CHAPTER SIX

'OH, DAMN!'

Vicki ripped the sheet of paper from the pad, screwed it up into a tight, angry ball and hurled it straight into the overflowing waste-paper bin. She mopped her brow, sticky in the afternoon heat. This was turning out to be the most demanding assignment she had ever struggled with, she thought gloomily, completely eclipsing the battles she had had with that low-fat spread, or even that world-shattering new-formula hair mousse which had sunk from the market without trace within six months. The copy for this brochure had to be diamond-brilliant, as polished as Proust, as scintillating as Oscar Wilde, as . . .

She sat, tapping her pen against the tip of her nose and staring across at the bookshelves opposite her. She would have preferred not to work in Gilles' study; the entire austere room was redolent of the man, of his formidable personality, while the slight citrus scent of his aftershave hung in the air, tantalising her nostrils and somehow getting between her and her task.

But that first morning, after giving her a lightning guided tour of the large creamery in the village below and the various meticulous stages which went into making a Laroque cheese and which she had, against her will, begun to find fascinating, Gilles had insisted that she work in here. It was as though, she thought resentfully, he wanted to be quite certain where she was at all times.

Still, at least, since that disquieting episode on the rug—momentarily her eyes strayed across to that same innocuous-looking sheepskin—he had been unfailingly formal and correct in his manner towards her each time they met, which in any case was only for meals. And after dinner each evening she had mumbled something about 'getting on' and retired to the study, though she always worked at the table now, and never sprawled out full-length on the rug.

Despite her anxieties about the brochure, the surging relief which she had felt when he had first suggested it had not at all dissipated. If anything, it had increased as she became engrossed in her work. In fact, she realised with a suddenness that took her quite by surprise, in spite of all the torn up papers and false starts and her very real concern as to whether the finished article would meet with Gilles' stern approbation, she was actually enjoying it.

She knew that she should be resentful that she was being kept here, still a virtual prisoner—even though when she went for short walks in the grounds now she felt instinctively that her 'tail' had been withdrawn, a sign that Gilles trusted her to that extent—but somehow the resentment had faded and a strange sensation which she had never experienced before was gently taking hold of her: not exactly tranquillity, but something like it. It helped, of course, that he no longer believed her to be a junkie . . . and yet, because he was seemingly as determined as ever to exact payment of her debt from her, he must still think she had been party to the fraud. Why else should he be keeping her here so determinedly? She shouldn't care a jot what his opinion of her was, but nevertheless that last thought gave her a strangely painful pang . . .

As though endowed with a will of their own, her eyes drifted back to the rug. Those insidious thoughts would keep creeping back, rapping at her mind for admittance. Supposing she had not come belatedly to her senses that evening, leapt back just in time from the abyss which Gilles had been sedulously beckoning her towards? What might have happened?... Strange, dangerously exciting fantasies were weaving themselves in and out of her brain... Just what would it be like to be made love to by——

'Stop it!' She spoke aloud, fiercely banging her knuckles against her forehead, and picked up her pen again... And yet, was she being foolish, denying herself an experience which, at twenty-four, she should be mature enough to handle—an experience which just might, with such a skilled lover as she felt certain he would be, remove once and for all the dark, tortured shadows which lurked always in her mind...? But might that not be tantamount to tearing apart an entire house to cure a leaking roof? That night, as she had slammed the door and rushed headlong to her room, the turbulence of feelings had rocked her almost physically, and she would not dare risk making herself prey to those perilous emotions again...

Vicki sighed heavily, then almost jumped clean out of her skin as a large hand came past her shoulder and scooped up the pad, now adorned with an elegant doodle that she had just been busily creating all over yet another fresh sheet of paper. She willed herself not to turn around.

'Hmm, most interesting. A design for a new Laroque logo, I presume.'

Gilles dropped the pad in front of her. She ripped off the despoiled sheet and crumpled it viciously between her fingers as though it were someone's face.

'I—I was thinking.'

'So I gather. But there is no need for you to justify yourself. I did not, I assure you, come to check up on your progress, Victoria——'

'Oh, for pity's sake,' the tension of having him stand barely a foot away from her put a savage bite into her voice, 'call me Vicki. Everyone else does.'

She scowled up at him, but he only shook his head decisively. 'I shall be the—what do you say?—exception to the rule. For myself, I prefer Victoria.'

'You would,' she muttered, only just inaudibly, and, pushing the chair back violently, she stood up.

'You have finished for today?'

'No. At least, I——' She drew a deep breath and felt some of the tension ebb gently from her. After all, it was understandable that he should be concerned about the work, and if she became too scratchy he would no doubt be happy to make things even more difficult for her. 'I've decided to scrap what I did yesterday. I want to make this brochure completely different from your usual supermarket pamphlet, however high-class.'

She pursed her lips, trying to put into words the idea which, after bubbling softly in her mind since she woke that morning, had suddenly crystallised. 'This is a really beautiful valley.' She looked directly up at him and was surprised by some fleeting expression which was gone before she could put a name to it. 'Well, I'll make use of that. You told me at the creamery that it's the lush meadows and pastures, the particular blend of wild flowers and grasses that makes the milk of your sheep so rich and so individual.

'So we'll capitalise on that—not on the fact that you can produce X tonnes a year, or even that your cheese is increasingly sought after by French gourmets, et cetera, et cetera. I'm going to begin right at the beginning—with your pastures, your sheep.' She gave him a sudden, impish grin. 'Maybe we could even give Casanova a starring role. Anyway, I'll stroll on up there now—see if I can pick out some likely shots for when the photographer comes.'

He shook his head again. 'You cannot walk in this heat. I will drive you there.'

She tapped her foot in silent exasperation. An afternoon in close contact with Gilles? This wasn't what she'd planned, not in the least. 'Oh, no, I'd rather not—I mean, that won't be necessary,' she began agitatedly. 'I like the heat, and besides, Monique has given me a straw hat——'

He held up his hand to silence her. 'You must stop fighting me, Victoria.' Then, as she glowered at him, nonplussed, he went on reflectively, 'You are perhaps right, though. It will be helpful for you to see the entire process, but we shall commence, not with the pastures but with the maturing stage. You will, I think, find it interesting.'

Interesting? Row upon row of Laroque specials in some musty warehouse . . .

'And then I will drive you up into the hills, so you may go and fetch your sunhat.'

Vicki, clutching the pad to her, gazed stubbornly at him across the table. Maybe if she held her ground she might emerge as the victor of this latest little tussle of wills, just as she had won that other one. But those eyes...deep, deep blue eyes that you could drown in—or even, she thought with a spurt of near panic, that you could sink in without trace. And now, they were flashing her a clear message. Perhaps, after all, she would let him win this time.

'All right,' she conceded graciously. 'It is rather hot.'

He nodded gravely—after all, he was too big a man, in every way, to allow the slightest flicker of triumph to show. 'I will wait for you outside.'

The track rose steadily towards the mountains, but after only half a mile or so Gilles pulled up the Land Rover, clambered out and set off along a narrow path which led seemingly right into the flank of the hillside. Vicki, following him, saw with astonishment that directly ahead of them, barring their way, was a massive if rather ramshackle wooden door. He fished out a large key from the pocket of his jeans and the door swung back, revealing a high, dark tunnel.

Just inside, on a shelf, was a row of hurricane lamps and he lit one. As he adjusted the flame, he remarked over his shoulder, 'I'm having an electricity generator installed, but until then——' He took up the lamp, then turned to Vicki, who was still hovering uncertainly in the entrance, feeling the cold, humid air unroll itself like a sinuous snake to meet her. 'Come.'

The flaring circle of golden light illuminated Gilles and the first few feet of the tunnel. Beyond, there was absolute darkness. Vicki, her heart pounding, felt her skin crawl, but before she could frame the determined 'No' he had taken a firm hold of her hand and was steering her unwilling feet down into the darkness.

'Why have you brought me here?'

She was panting to keep up with his long stride, but, 'You will see,' was his only reply. The tunnel, so narrow in places that her shoulder brushed against its clammy walls, was winding downhill at a steep angle. They must be almost at the very core of the mountain, millions of tons of rock between them and the sunlight . . .

She stopped dead, jerking Gilles to a standstill also. 'I don't like it,' she said in a small, constrained voice, which echoed horribly off the tunnel walls. 'I c-can't go any further.'

Her teeth were chattering, her whole body was shivering; she pressed her knuckles to her mouth in a futile effort to control herself. Dimly, she saw Gilles set down the blurred halo of lamp, and then he had taken her into his arms, cradling her tightly against him, rocking her as though she were a child in need of comfort. She could feel the strength of his body flowing into her, so that at length the trembling ceased and he eased her gently away from him.

'Quite recovered?' He gave her a warm, beautiful smile, and all at once her legs began to tremble again, but not this time from fear of the dark tunnel.

'Quite recovered,' she managed to say. She tried imperceptibly to edge away from him, but his hand still held her firmly, his eyes fixed on her upturned face.

'I will take you out if you wish, but I promise you we are almost there. Shall we go on?'

She nodded, even summoning a faint smile. He picked up the lamp and, before she could guess what he was going to do, slid his other arm firmly around her waist, drawing her close to him, and set off, but this time keeping carefully in step with her smaller strides. Now that all the fear and tension had erupted in that uncontrollable outburst, she was beginning to feel deeply embarrassed and ashamed of her weakness.

'I'm sorry—about getting in such a state, I mean.'

Her voice was husky, less from the effect of the cold air on her lungs than the nearness of Gilles. Their two selves were so close that her body was aware of every movement of his—the tensing of the muscles as he walked, the tautness of his arm encircling her waist—as though it were her own.

'Please, Victoria.' His voice held no scorn. 'Do not apologise. It is I who am at fault. Many people are afraid of caves, of confined spaces—I should have asked you.'

She laughed wryly. 'I didn't know I was. I've never fancied pot-holing or anything, but I've never reacted like that before.'

In the half-darkness she frowned to herself. What had brought on this sudden fear? Was it perhaps another manifestation of her insecurity, her unhappiness, brought on by the drawn-out trauma with David which had made her for so long feel that her personality was almost physically fraying at the edges, unravelling like a piece of discarded knitting . . .?

But this was no time for indulging in yet another bout of self-analysis—or self-pity. Ahead, the passage had widened out, and when Gilles held up the lamp she saw that they were in an enormous cave, lined with row upon row of slatted wooden shelves on which stood hundreds of round, pale gold cheeses.

He laughed at her astonished face. 'You said you wished to see all the processes. Well, this is the final stage. The curds are brought up here, already shaped, then they are injected with the mould spores which produce the blue veins, and then the air in the cave, which filters down through fissures in the rock,' Vicki glanced up and saw, miles above her head, or so it seemed, some tiny star points of light, 'brings about the miracle which creates *le fromage Laroque*, whose virtues you will so eloquently extol!'

Taking up a slim steel tube, he deftly drove it into the heart of one of the cheeses, twisted it slightly then withdrew it. He tapped out a small roll of cheese into his hand, sniffed it, nodded slightly, then broke off a piece and popped it into her mouth. As it met her tongue she tasted its strength and the salty undertone to it, but then, as she tentatively chewed, it melted to a delicately creamy sweetness.

'Mmm. It's delicious.' She licked away a last crumb from the corner of her mouth and he laughed.

'I'm glad it finds favour with you. After all, as a vegetarian, you are presumably quite a connoisseur of cheeses.'

He dug a piece of chalk from his pocket, inscribed a symbol on the end of the shelf, then humped the cheese he had sampled under one arm and picked up the lamp. 'You shall have more of this at dinner tonight. The rest will be in our Paris and Madrid outlets by the end of the week.'

Once back in the Land Rover, the precious cheese cushioned in a box of straw, they headed further up into the mountains, the narrow track rapidly becoming so steep that it seemed that nothing less than a four-wheel-drive goat could possibly get up it! But Gilles, his hands tensed on the steering-wheel, skilfully coaxed every ounce of power out of the protesting vehicle until, ahead of them, flanked by a wide belt of pines, were the high, rolling pastures. Down below, the lush spring grass had long since faded to the dullness of late summer, but up here, nourished by the mountain rains, the grass was still fresh, its peppermint green sprinkled with wild flowers. Everywhere were sheep, the spring crop of lambs almost as large as the ewes.

Rather stiffly, Vicki eased herself out of her seat, then stood absolutely still, knocked weak-kneed by the breathtaking beauty. A lump formed in her throat—it was so lovely up here, so remote, so peaceful. She became aware that Gilles was watching her across the Land Rover, his eyes intent on her. His gaze was, as so often, inscrutable, and yet all at once she felt uncomfortable, as though her deep, instinctive emotion had been laid open for his inspection. She hastily smoothed away the enraptured expression.

'You like it?' His voice was perfectly casual, but she sensed behind the words an undercurrent which only increased her unease.

She nodded slowly. 'Yes. It's wonderful——'

'In early summer it is even better. Then all these pastures for miles are first thick with daffodils, and a little later they become a sheet of buttercups and wild orchids.'

'And yet——' She broke off.

'And yet?'

She glanced over her shoulder. All but forgotten in her pleasure at the pastures, the mountains were now crowding in again, their jagged peaks seeming to frown threateningly at her. Something of the sensation of almost human hostility she had experienced that day she had fled up into them flickered in her again, brushing across her skin so that she could feel the goose-bumps. First the cave, now the mountains—really, what a spineless jellyfish she was turning into! But she could not prevent herself looking at him, almost pleadingly.

'It's the mountains. I don't like them.'

Gilles' lips twisted slightly, but he only said, 'It is because of your fear when you were lost.'

She pondered, biting on her lip. 'No,' she said slowly. 'It's not that. I think it's because they're so new to me. I come from Lincolnshire—that's a part of England that's very flat, though it's beautiful—marvellous, enormous skies, especially in winter. I find all this,' she gestured towards the mountains without looking at them, 'rather—not exactly frightening—but it disturbs me.' She pulled a sheepish, apologetic face. 'I feel as though they're watching me.'

'But Victoria,' Gilles banged the door to with unnecessary violence, 'the mountains, those peaks are a part of my valley—after all, without them, there would *be* no valley.'

He strode off, almost as though he were trying to leave her behind, and she had to run to catch up with him. But gradually his pace eased, and he gave her a faint, enigmatic smile, then took her hand and led her across the meadow towards a small wooden hut, tucked against the shelter of massive boulders.

'This is where some of my shepherds live in the summer months. We drive the sheep up here every spring, as soon as most of the snows of winter have melted, and they stay up here until autumn, then we bring them back down to the lowland pastures. We hold a *fête* in the village square that night—it is a pity you will not be here then——' there was a momentary undercurrent in his tone, which she did not quite manage to interpret '—for you would enjoy it, I think. Many of the people still dress in the old costume and there is dancing, singing—and plenty of our local wine, of course. Each summer we have a fine crop of new babies,' he added with wry amusement.

'Oh,' Vicki laughed but could not quite meet his eye.

Two men were approaching, the same two, she realised, who had gone off that day with Gilles in pursuit of the ram. He shook hands casually with them, they nodded courteously to her, then the three launched into a rapid conversation which she did not even try to follow. She caught the word 'Casanova' from Gilles, and the two men's open grins made her grateful for her incomprehension, but then he turned to her.

'You would like to meet him—Casanova?'

'Well, I'm——' she began, but, leaving the two men to return to their hut, he took her arm and steered her across the field towards a clump of hawthorn bushes, their berries reddening with the approach of autumn. In their shade, a dozen or so sheep were lolling around an enormous, barrel-chested ram, his heavy, shaggy fleece and tightly curled yellow horns giving him a disturbingly pagan air. If ever there was a bull in sheep's clothing, she thought involuntarily, this was he.

'Well, what do you think of him?'

Vicki stared at the beast, then looked up at Gilles, her eyes dancing. 'He looks very—smug.'

He snorted with open amusement, and the ram favoured them both with a cold stare. 'So he should. After all, he is the pampered lord of an adoring harem. What more could any male wish for?'

'Hmm.' She studied the animal thoughtfully. 'You know,' she said slowly, at last, 'he reminds me very much of you.'

She finished on a little gasp of trepidation. The words had seemed to tumble out of their own accord. Whatever imp of devilment was getting into her today—and how would he, totally unpredictable as he was, react to this newfound pertness?

Gilles, though, put back his head, exposing the strong, tanned column of his throat, and gave a shout of laughter, so, emboldened, she went on recklessly, 'He's as tough as that granite boulder over there, strong, proud—no, utterly conceited.' She was beginning to thoroughly enjoy herself, the laughter bubbling through her like oxygen in the sparkling mountain air.

'Take care, Victoria.' He held up a finger in not altogether mock warning.

'And besides,' Vicki, swept along by her own momentum, was quite unable to rein herself in, 'he's giving me an even nastier look than you've ever managed, which is saying a great——'

With a yelp of terror she sprang back as Gilles made a determined grab for her, then turned and ran, scattering startled woolly bodies all round her.

'Hey, don't frighten the sheep!' There was real exasperation in his yell.

She half hesitated, half turned, then, as from out of the corner of her eye she saw him set off in pursuit, she fled in a frantic zigzag course across the hillside, a feeling of delicious terror filling her. Gilles was so much stronger than her. On the other hand, she was much smaller and therefore lighter on her feet... Still, she couldn't keep running for ever, and when she stopped . . .

Just ahead, a wide, rock-strewn stream was catapulting itself headlong towards the valley. Without pulling up in the slightest, she crossed it, leaping from stone to stone, and landed on the far side with a gasp of relief.

But at that same instant, Gilles' outstretched fingertips brushed against the back of her blouse, then closed on the thin fabric. She jerked forward violently to break his grip, lost her balance and tumbled flat on her face in the lush grass, bringing him heavily down beside her.

CHAPTER SEVEN

THE DENSE grass had cushioned her fall but still she lay winded, her face buried, her breath sobbing against her ribs. She felt Gilles cautiously ease himself up, then he was raising her by the shoulders to a sitting position.

'Are you hurt?'

She turned, to see very real concern puckering his brow, then drew in a final gasping breath as she shook her head. 'No.'

She regarded his anxious face for a moment, her lips twitching, then quite suddenly burst out laughing, a joyous, marvellous, unrestrained laugh, the sort which her body had almost forgotten how to produce. It felt as though a key was turning in a rusty lock, the seized-up hinges yielding, first reluctantly, then gratefully.

Stretching back her head and shoulders, she arched her neck as she luxuriated in the strange feeling which was irradiating her. What was it—this strange, bewildering sensation? Could it possibly be—*happiness*?

Gilles was watching her thoughtfully. 'You know, that is the first time I have ever seen you laugh. You are pretty when you smile, which heaven knows is seldom enough, but when you laugh——'

She wanted to move away, but his dark gaze was holding her motionless, the expression in his eyes doing strange things to her breathing, almost as though she were still winded by that tumble. Her own eyes flickered and fell to the pulse at the base of his throat which, just beneath the skin, was beating erratic time, as though keeping in step with her own fluttering heartbeat.

Very gently he took her hand. She thought he was going to kiss it, but instead he pressed it, palm inward, against his chest, and under the heel of her hand she felt the strong yet rapid contraction and relaxation of the muscle, its beat crossing the barrier of cotton and flesh between them, so that she could have sworn it was his heart that was pounding in her ears.

'Victoria.' His voice was soft.

'Yes?' It was hardly more than a tiny sigh, and she sensed him lean forward intently to catch it.

'Look at me.' The command was still gentle, yet inexorable.

No longer possessing a will of her own, she raised her eyes to meet his. For a long breath they stared at each other, then with infinite slowness he slid his fingers beneath her arms, lifting her up to him to meet his kiss. His mouth moved across hers, his lips brushing to and fro in gentle, hypnotic seduction, then slid down across her throat, lingering over her flickering pulse.

With one hand, he moved aside the collar of her blouse and buried his face against the curve of her neck, the very tip of his tongue moving in tiny, erotic circles against her tender flesh. She was lost in his arms, his warm, alive maleness filling her whole being, until she was almost suffocating, caught up in a wildly swirling spiral of totally new sensations.

When she felt his hand on the button of her blouse, she sagged against him in mute appeal, then the blouse was pulled aside and his warm fingertips were sweeping against the firm swell of her breasts, above the prim white cotton of the borrowed bra. He held her away from him slightly, then her breasts were freed. She heard his breath catch in his throat; his hand cupped one breast, curving possessively over the soft, creamy-pale mound, his fingers tracing an unhurried path round and round to the very centre of the maze. His skin brushed against the peak, so lightly that she almost felt the whorl of print at his finger-ends, yet at that infinitesimal touch it sprang hardening into life.

Her whole body was seized by an intense, racking shudder. Someone, surely not herself, gave a tiny, yearning sob, then her arms went round him, her hands locking on fistfuls of shirt and muscled back, as she was lost to everything beyond the double circle of their arms.

Gilles lifted his head for a moment and looked directly at her. His face was flushed and she saw, in the intense blue-black depths of his eyes, beyond her own tiny pinpoint reflection, desire. But there was also, she realised, something else, something which made her stiffen suddenly as her throat tightened in panic. Beyond the desire she had glimpsed warm tenderness—and fear came, freezing, swift. She must draw back before it was too late, for this new, totally unexpected expression was altogether more dangerous than mere predatory physical desire, because—why? She asked herself the question and knew the answer in the same fleeting instant. Because tenderness might come to threaten the whole edifice on which she had so painfully reconstructed her life, after David had gone.

She loosed her grip and pushed herself clear of him in a sudden jack-knife movement. But before she could quite escape his hands had fastened on her, those tender fingers now almost burning through her skin in barely suppressed violence, and jerking her back towards him.

'No, Gilles—please!' The cry burst from her as he shook her and, terrified, she was forced to stare into his angry face. 'I—I'm sorry, but please, no,' she repeated.

His eyes held hers for a long moment, then his lips tightened and his hands dropped from her. 'You know, Victoria,' there were splinters of ice in that ruthlessly controlled voice, 'promise and tease—that is a dangerous occupation for a young girl to pursue. One day you may meet a man who is less—forbearing than I, and more inclined for the ugliness of rape.'

She sat motionless, her head bent, her face hidden. 'I'm s-sorry.' Her voice shook. 'I didn't mean to, but——' She broke off, desperate for him to understand. 'I—I don't want to get involved like that, not ever again.'

Her tone was empty now, the desolate sadness washing through her, a grey sea, bringing only wretchedness. She bit fiercely on her lip in an effort to keep back the tears which threatened, but a huge one spilled over on to her cheek, and, when she lifted an unsteady hand to brush it quickly away before Gilles saw it and piled even more contempt on her, she only succeeded in flicking it off to land with a tiny plop on the knee of his faded blue denims.

The next instant, with a half-angry, half-tender, wholly incoherent exclamation, he had pulled her to him. 'Don't cry, *chérie*,' he said into her hair, but the softened tone, the unexpected term of endearment, acted on her overwrought emotions like salt on a raw wound, and she put her head against his strong chest and wept.

'This man—your husband.' Vicki tensed, both at the words and at the tone of open anger in Gilles' voice. 'What has he done to you? Not only has he walked out on you, but he has hurt you—damaged you greatly.'

She knew that she should leap to David's defence—it was absolutely no concern of Gilles'. And yet, why should she? The old bitterness welled up in her like poisonous bile. David, despite his outer softness, had used her with a ruthless selfishness, and then, when things hadn't worked out as he'd planned, had, as Gilles so bluntly put it, walked out on her, leaving her to collapse into a morass of depression and darkness from which she had still not emerged back into the light.

But the tears at least had stopped; Gilles gently raised her to her feet and regarded her with a slightly crooked smile. 'You know the saying—anything worth having is well worth waiting for.' Very deliberately, he lifted one hand and brushed his thumb across her full lower lip. 'I promise you, *ma petite*, that when you are finally free from this hurt, and one day you will be, it will be very worth while indeed to be around!'

His voice was light, yet the unspoken meaning in his eyes made her colour poppy-crimson. But then, as she looked at him uncertainly, he ruffled her hair softly and said, 'Come, it is time for us to return.'

As they recrossed the stream, rather more carefully this time, and retraced their way through the meadows, her brain was seething. *Never!* In her fit of anger and fear in his study, she had hurled that word at him. And surely that brutal 'never' had to stand? The faintest weakening, the slightest compromise would be disastrous—if not for him, certainly for her. She had to get the brochure finished as soon as humanly possible. That was the answer—the only answer.

Gilles was walking beside her, in that easy, loping stride of one quite accustomed to covering distances which would floor an ordinary man. She shot him a tentative look from beneath her damp lashes. How strong, how handsome he was. To think that once, and that so very recently, she had airily assured herself that she did not find him in the least attractive. What a self-deluding idiot she'd been! Why, he breathed sensual, animal attraction from every pore, not deliberately but as an inescapable part of himself.

And not only self-deluding, she thought, as she climbed into the Land Rover, but self-denying, too. It would—it should have been so simple for her to abandon herself in his sensuality, discover herself in the power of his love—and be miraculously restored to a whole person again ... And yet, if Gilles should learn the entire truth ... Her mind and her body flinched from the questions, the anger that she knew must inevitably follow. No, she thought bleakly. It should have been—but would that it were so easy!

Finished! Vicki pushed away the completed mock-up of the brochure and sat back in the leather chair, releasing a long sigh of mingled satisfaction and relief. That morning, the photographer had delivered the prints of the shots she had supervised, and she had worked non-stop since then, marrying the illustrations to her copy.

She stared pensively down at it. All it needed was Gilles' approval and it could be sent off to the printer. Her job was over. These few sheets were her exit visa out of the valley. Now he would be able to keep her here no longer—he would have to let her go. And surely, after that abortive encounter up in the pastures four days previously, he would be as eager as she to open the cage door.

Since then, she had worked in a frenzy—though whether that frenzy had been inspired by a spurt of creative genius, or just sheer trembling anxiety to be away once and for all, she would not allow herself to ponder. But at least he couldn't expect her to wait to see it through the printers... Although it was a pity in a way that she would never see the finished product.

Never see it! The pang that ran through her took her completely by surprise. After all, she told herself, in just a day or so she really would be free of her captor and safely back in London. And yet, strangely, the elation she should be feeling was altogether missing. But maybe she was being a shade premature anyway, for she had not yet humbly submitted the work for her lord and master's seal of approval...

She heard his voice in the passage just outside the study. Talk of the devil and he was sure to appear! Gathering up the papers, she went out. Gilles, who was deep in conversation with the housekeeper, lifted one enquiring eyebrow in her direction, wound up what he was saying and turned to her.

She thrust the sheets at him. 'It's done. I've finished it.'

'You have finished it,' he repeated slowly.

When she nodded, he took them from her and gestured her back into the study, closing the door behind them. Without another word, he sat at the desk, spread the papers in front of him and, swivelling gently to and fro, began studying them intently.

Vicki stood across the desk from him, vainly scanning his bent face for any reaction—the least sign of enthusiasm. For a fleeting second she had a vision of herself ten years previously, a schoolgirl standing by her headmaster's desk, anxiously awaiting his approbation for an essay she had had to write as punishment for some long-forgotten misdemeanour.

But then, as she continued to gaze at him, a very different and far more alarming feeling welled up in her. Quite suddenly, she wanted to cradle that oblivious dark head to her, stroke it, twine her fingers in the black, thick hair. Her hands were already moving when, fiercely catching herself up, she thrust them deep into the pockets of her denim skirt.

At last, after an uncomfortably long interval, Gilles set down the final sheet and looked up at her, unsmiling.

'Well?' she demanded, her belligerence masking, she hoped, her growing uncertainty. 'It's all right, isn't it?'

He grunted non-committally and she stared at him. She certainly couldn't do the work any better—she knew that—so if he wasn't satisfied . . . The needles of anxiety pricking at her mind gave an even greater sharpness to her voice.

'It meets with your approval, I trust?' She had not, of course, expected him to turn somersaults of delight around the room in an orgy of unrestrained Gallic enthusiasm; just as well, she thought sourly, but at least he might have the grace—no, the common decency, to look just slightly impressed by her prowess. 'Well, thank you, Victoria, for all your hard work. You've made an excellent job of it,' she said tartly.

He eyed her coolly. 'You said it would take you two weeks.'

'What? Oh, yes.' She waved a dismissive hand. 'Well, it happens like that sometimes. I can take a week, a month over something, or, like a bolt from the blue, the inspiration comes and it's done. When I said a fortnight, I was just covering myself—and it wouldn't be any better if I'd taken any longer,' she added emphatically.

She paused to weigh up his reaction, but his face was still devoid of expression so she pressed on. 'So now, if you'd be kind enough to take me to Toulouse, or get someone else to——'

He frowned. 'Toulouse?'

'Yes, to the British consul, to arrange a temporary passport.'

A faint smile flickered across his thin lips. 'I'm so sorry to disabuse you, Victoria, but there is no British consul in Toulouse.'

She gaped at him, momentarily taken aback. So much for her earlier efforts to escape; even if she'd managed to reach the city, she'd only have been stranded there.

'Well, you'll just have to get me to the nearest one.' The appalling thought of being stuck in an alien town, penniless and alone, had put an even more biting edge to her voice. 'Perhaps it's escaped your notice, but as well as no passport, I've got no money. I'll have to arrange a loan from them—after all, they do repatriate in a dire emergency, and this *is* one.'

'That will not be necessary.'

'What do you mean?'

'There will be no need for you to borrow money.'

'Why not?' She looked at him suspiciously. What devious plan was he hatching this time?

'I accept that you were not a party to the fraud perpetrated on Jeanne——'

'Oh, and what's brought on this sudden, miraculous change of heart?'

'I know you sufficiently well now to be sure that, however naïve or unwise you may be in your choice of companions, you are essentially honest.'

'Well, thank you so much!' Vicki's pent-up temper finally boiled over. 'And thank you for the unsolicited character reference. May I ask how long ago you came to this conclusion? You've kept it very carefully to yourself—long enough to make absolutely sure I finished your brochure, at any rate. I was right—the age of serfdom isn't over in this valley,' she went on recklessly. 'Cheap labour, that's all I've been.'

'Be silent.' Gilles' voice was dangerously quiet, and there was a flush of dusky red along his tanned cheekbones. 'If you had not let your caustic tongue be so precipitate, I would have told you that I intend to pay you, and pay you well, for this work.' He tapped the brochure. 'But first, you will undertake one more task for me.'

'Oh, no, I won't!' She was almost shouting. 'You're not moving the goalposts at this stage.' He gave her a coldly interrogative stare. 'Changing the rules, reneging on our deal,' she elaborated. 'You've had your pound of flesh, and now you admit belatedly that I was innocent all along. I've done your bloody brochure, as I said I would, and I'm leaving.'

He pushed back the chair and stood up abruptly. 'You will leave when I say so. May I remind you,' he was clearly keeping his voice even with an immense effort, 'that you are still in no position to dictate terms to me? You have no clothes, no money, no passport. Sit down, and I will tell you what you are going to do.'

Vicki drummed her fingers in a furious tattoo on the desk, but behind her mutinous scowl was total perplexity. She desperately longed for the luxury of hurling a few unpalatable home truths at her adversary, then turning on her heel to make a haughty exit, but some frayed remnants of common sense held her in check.

Her eyes fell on the brochure lying between them. At least, if he was intent on cheating her, he wouldn't have that. But even as her fingers moved to snatch the sheets of paper and rip them into useless shreds, Gilles, quicker than thought, had seized them. He slid open the top drawer, dropped them into it, turned the key and thrust it into his jeans pocket.

Her revenge frustrated, Vicki regarded him with undisguised loathing. 'You really are a five-star swine,' she said at last, her voice shaking.

'But of course.' Now that he was so securely in command of the situation he could afford to relax, she thought malevolently, even allow that faint tinge of amusement which so set her teeth on edge to creep into his voice.

'If you want another brochure,' she said icily, 'you can just forget it. I—I'd cut my right arm off before I do any more copy for——'

'Has anyone ever told you how beautiful you are when you are angry? Those grey eyes flashing fire, the way you toss your hair back. Now,' he went on as, shocked into open-mouthed silence, she could only gape at him again, 'sit down.' He waved her towards a chair.

'Thank you, but I prefer to stand,' she said stubbornly. The longing to implant a few well-placed bruises on that implacable face was growing fast, only the thought of the instant retribution holding her back.

'Sit down, or——' He left the threat unfinished, but she sank into the chair, her only final, tiny act of defiance being to fold her arms and stare sullenly at the floor.

Gilles, though, made no effort to sit. He walked round the desk, then leaned against it so that, out of the corner of her eye, she could see his long legs casually crossed, almost brushing against her own.

'Now—you will listen to me, with no outbursts. And if you still harbour any thoughts of physically assaulting me,' Vicki's nails curled into her upper arms, 'well, we both know that you would be very unwise to try.'

He paused, but she kept her eyes firmly on the beige tweed carpet, as though transfixed by its beauty, and he went on, 'There is, as I told you, no British consul in Toulouse, but there is one in Bordeaux, and I shall take you there tomorrow.'

Vicki's eyes leapt to his face. Had she, after all, misjudged him? Perhaps he'd just been stringing her along, after all, enjoying her reaction, playing her as a fisherman might play a trout, to feed his own devious brand of humour.

She was still trying to subdue her face into lines of chastened humility when he went on. 'The fact that there is a consul in Bordeaux is a fortunate coincidence, for I had already planned that you should go there with me.' She stared at him, stupefied by the easy confidence of his words. 'A two-day convention is being held there on new methods of dealing with the surpluses in the dairy industries, and we are going to attend it.'

She leapt to her feet in disbelief. 'But that's impossible. I don't know anything about dairy conferences, for heaven's sake. I'm a——'

'That is immaterial. There will be English people there, valuable contacts. You will be of use to me——'

'It's quite ridiculous.' She shook her head in total bewilderment. 'You don't need me. You speak perfect English.'

'Let us just say, then,' there was a crisp edge of irritation in his voice, 'that I intend that you will be there with me. I shall pay you, of course, for your services, in addition to the brochure, and you will also gain your passport.'

'Oh, yes: first the stick, now the carrot.'

'Your clothes,' he went on as if she hadn't spoken, his eyes flicking with apparent uninterest over her body and taking in the simple T-shirt and denim skirt, 'are wholly unsuitable. I shall take you into Toulouse this afternoon to remedy that.'

'You'll have to give me the money you owe me, then.'

'I shall buy them for you——'

'No, thanks, I'd rather——'

'—and if you wish,' he continued smoothly, 'you can regard them as part-payment.'

He was playing with her, she knew that, secure in the knowledge that she had to submit. The unwelcome picture came involuntarily to her mind of herself as that fish, wriggling helplessly on a line as the fisherman—Gilles—slowly, inexorably drew her in towards him . . .

Part-payment—for what exactly? Her eyes darkened with horrified suspicion, but at the same moment he went on, 'And you do not need to worry your head on that score, *ma petite*. When I made our hotel reservation, I specified two single rooms, with their own bathrooms of course, so that sets all your fears at rest, I trust.'

'You've made a booking—for me?' she repeated mechanically. Then, as the full realisation hit her, 'You booked my room, without even bothering to find out if I was prepared to come with you.'

Her voice rose several notches, but he only glanced at his watch. 'If I am taking you to Toulouse after lunch, then I must go down to the creamery now.' He eyed her skimpy T-shirt with disfavour. 'Go and change into something marginally more suited to town.' He straightened up and sauntered over to the door. 'I shall see you later, then,' he said over his shoulder.

Vicki slammed her fists down against the desk. 'But I haven't said that I'll come with you—to Toulouse or Bordeaux, or—or anywhere,' she hurled despairingly at his retreating back.

CHAPTER EIGHT

GILLES pushed open the heavy glass door with the name 'Roxanne' in discreet gilt lettering at one corner, and a blast of expensively perfumed air came wafting out to meet them. A woman, slim and chic in black, who had been attending to a well-dressed elderly woman, abruptly abandoned her to a young assistant and advanced on them across the soft, springy carpet. She greeted Gilles, the watchful Vicki noted sardonically, with graceful deference, then, after a swift, all-professional assessment of the simple dark Provençal cotton, Vicki herself, with marginally less respect.

Vicki was forced to stand, staring rather glumly around her, while they discussed her, Gilles relating in vague terms how she had mislaid all her luggage and was in urgent need of some appropriate clothes for a working visit to Bordeaux. The woman, whom he introduced as Madame Jaubert, gave Vicki another coolly appraising glance—then, having settled Gilles, looking rather incongruous despite his beautifully cut lightweight grey suit and white silk shirt, on a small antique pink velvet chaise-longue, set off with Vicki in tow.

She riffled swiftly through the clothes on the first rail and fetched out an armful of dresses. 'If *mademoiselle* would come this way.'

The note almost of subservience in her voice rasped on Vicki. That obsequiousness was all for Gilles, lounging there on that ridiculous little sofa, his long legs casually stretched out before him—none of it was for her. Well, she would just have to assert herself, show this woman that she was more than merely an obedient, mindless puppet.

Putting her hand on the discreet price tag of the dress nearest her, she turned it over, then closed her eyes momentarily as she caught sight of the horrendous row of noughts. She had been determined that, at the very least, Gilles would not pay for her clothes—she would send him a cheque to cover every penny. But with these dresses, even crossing off most of the noughts, it meant——

Anger rose in her. She'd been making for one of the less expensive chain stores; it was Gilles who had relentlessly steered her unwilling feet towards the discreetly sophisticated windows of Roxanne, and now this atmosphere, so redolent of money and opulence, was throwing her totally off balance.

'Pardon, madame,' She snatched the dress and, carrying it at arm's length, advanced on Gilles.

'Look,' she said with no preamble, 'I'm not having any of these clothes. They're far too expensive. *Eight hundred pounds* for a dress!' Her voice shook slightly, even having to say the words.

He shrugged. 'That is not your problem.'

Vicki's lips tightened. 'You know I said on the way down here that I intend paying you back for them, and you——'

'And I said, we shall see—and now we do see,' he cut in laconically.

'Besides,' she went on, determined not to be put off, 'these dresses are in wool—they'll be far too warm. I need cotton——'

The manageress had appeared at her elbow, and Gilles shot Vicki a warning look before saying, in a tone of finality, 'In Bordeaux you will be representing Laroque Enterprises, therefore you will of course wear our products.'

'*Your* products?'

As she frowned in bewilderment, he hooked a finger into the neckline of the dress that she was dangling before him and drew out the sewn-in label. 'Laroque Pyrénéan.' Then, as she continued to stare uncomprehendingly, he went on impatiently, 'You surely realised that our main concern is wool? Laroque wool is renowned for its purity and fineness of texture—it has been the foundation of our family's wealth for over three centuries.'

'But the cheese——?'

His snort of laughter did not quite drown Madame Jaubert's shocked intake of breath.

'The cheese is merely a recent addition, a—what do you say?—sideline. I was somewhat—' he spread his hands '—bored, so I decided to diversify somewhat.'

Of course. A man of his restless energy and drive—it was hardly to be supposed that he would be content merely to follow in the well-trodden paths of previous generations of Laroques, however lucrative those paths might be. Even so, there was no valid reason that she could see why she should be a Laroque clothes-horse if she didn't so choose.

'Look,' she began, in a slightly more placatory tone, 'I'm sorry, but they just aren't the sort of things I wear. Apart from anything else,' she eyed the dress's slim lines, 'I don't like fitted clothes. I prefer loose, baggy——'

'But *mademoiselle*,' the manageress was clearly deeply distressed, 'with a superb young figure like yours, to wear loose——' she hesitated, clearly quite unable even to bring herself to pronounce the word 'baggy' '—clothes...'

Gilles shot Vicki another swift, speaking look that made her draw her breath unsteadily as, miserably angry, she stood between them. Yet again, there was nothing she could do. He had backed her into another corner and, apart from physically attacking him like a cornered rat, something which would have done a great deal for her self-esteem but very little to relieve her situation, there was no way out for her except to obediently toe the Laroque line.

Madame Jaubert, scenting victory, took the dress from Vicki's unresisting hand. 'If *mademoiselle* will follow me...'

The spacious, velvet-curtained changing-room was mirror-walled, the shaded lights throwing a cunningly flattering glow over Vicki as she turned slowly to glimpse yet another reflection of a creamy-skinned stranger, slim and delicate in the wisp of black dress which had that subtle cling which only French tailoring could achieve.

'And *mademoiselle* will agree, I am sure, that the fabric is not at all too warm. Monsieur Laroque brought in a textile designer some years ago, and he succeeded in marrying a silk thread with the wool.'

Vicki could only nod. It was true; the dress felt as light and cool on her body as air.

'And now, if *mademoiselle* will permit, for a dress like this, the hair should be worn—so.' The woman lifted Vicki's heavy chestnut hair, piling it up to leave her neck and shoulders free. 'These others,' she gestured to a straight soft turquoise dress and another in palest apricot with a matching jacket, 'being simpler day-dresses, are quite suited to *mademoiselle*'s present style.'

There was a faint something beneath the smoothly varnished words which was insidiously disturbing, and Vicki glanced up sharply. Meeting the woman's eyes in the mirror, she saw, fleetingly, under the bland impassiveness of her professional façade, an expression of—her own eyes widened in shock—scorn.

Instantly, she understood. Well, you *were* pretty slow on the uptake, she told her reflection fiercely, as the other woman turned away. It had been perfectly obvious from the moment they appeared that Gilles was a valued customer at Roxanne's, and as the shop did not, as far as she could see, sell a single item of menswear, that could only mean one thing. No wonder the manageress had given her such a thorough visual going-over. She, no doubt, was just the latest in a long line of Laroque women. How many others, she asked herself, as she began wriggling out of the black dress, had he escorted through these hallowed portals? Biting her lip, she turned for the woman to unzip her.

'But *mademoiselle*——' was there not even a scarcely veiled innuendo behind that harmless term, or was she becoming paranoid? '—will wish to show Monsieur Laroque the dresses she has chosen.'

'No, *mademoiselle* will not,' Vicki snapped, then reined herself in. Really, this place was bringing out hidden depths of nastiness she hadn't even realised she possessed, and, after all, she could hardly blame the woman for leaping to the wrong conclusion. She managed a pallid smile. 'But thank you for your help.'

The realisation of Madame Jaubert's automatic assumption had at least strengthened her resolve that, come hell or high water, she was going to pay for these clothes, even though it meant she was going to be in hock for months, if not years. Every other garment in her wardrobe would have to be sackcloth—in more ways than one—she thought grimly, as she remembered the state of her London bank account.

Even so, she acknowledged reluctantly, as she followed the manageress back into the shop, the woman had been right. Those garments, hanging shapelessly over her arm now, had done something utterly wonderful for her back there in the changing-room. Gilles watched her coming towards him, his face quite expressionless, as usual, but even though she sensed that he was noting the unaccustomed glow in her cheeks, the absurdly new way she was moving and holding her head, she could not stop herself. Oh, the effect of a few hanks of dirty sheep's wool, she thought, then hastily wiped away the faintly rueful smile.

'And now,' he said as they came up to him, 'you will need lingerie.'

Following his eyes, Vicki half turned and saw, on a gilt pedestal, cascades of cappuccino froth and lace. Just for a moment her will-power faltered, then she said firmly, 'Oh, no. I'll manage with what I've got.' And, conscious of the silent pricking of Madame Jaubert's ears, she added sweetly, 'After all, it's only for two working days.'

'As you wish,' Gilles nodded, graciously conceding defeat. 'But you must have shoes. You cannot continue to wear those disreputable objects.'

This time, Vicki was borne away to the tiny, highly select shoe department at the rear of the shop, to have her slim feet fitted out with a pair of beautiful Italian high-heeled pumps in black kid leather, with a matching bag, and another pair in creamy patent.

At the small gilt table—nothing so mercenary as a pay desk—no money or cheque-card changed hands, and as far as Vicki, glancing surreptitiously out of the corner of her eye, could see, Gilles merely scribbled an illegible signature across some sort of invoice. So he actually had an account at Roxanne's—she really was just the latest in an endless line. She was taken utterly by surprise by the sick pang which shot through her at the images which the knowledge conjured in her.

The young assistant brought out the frighteningly large pile of black- and gold-wrapped packages to the peacock-blue Renault Alpine turbo, which Gilles had casually left outside in direct contravention of any parking regulations, and then retreated.

He handed her in, got in beside her and was about to ease the powerful car out into the flow of traffic when the girl came running back, clutching another large box. He wound down his window and she thrust it in.

'*Madame* sends her apologies,' she gasped. 'She almost forgot this.'

He dropped the box on to Vicki's lap, slipped the car into gear and drove off.

'But I'm sure there's been some mistake,' Vicki protested, holding the package gingerly. 'We brought out all my things, I'm sure we did. Or is it something for you?' Maybe, after all, there was a men's department, tucked away in some discreet corner.

She looked at him enquiringly, but all he said was, 'No, I don't think so. But perhaps you had better open it and see.'

Something in his voice alerted her, but his expression was perfectly bland, so she turned instead to the black and gold string, undoing the knot with a final tweak and easing off the lid. She burrowed into the white tissue paper, then her fingers stilled. Under her hands, soft and fragile as a cobweb, was a mound of silk. Disbelievingly, she half drew out a tiny ivory lace bra then, her cheeks scarlet, she dropped it and rammed on the box lid before flinging it on to the rear seat as though its smooth luxury was contaminating her.

'I told you I don't want them. You can take them back right away, do you hear? I *won't* wear them!'

'That is a pity.' Gilles' eyes were carefully on the slow-moving file of traffic ahead and his voice was a lazy drawl. 'I shall want you to be completely at ease in Bordeaux, and I have always been given to understand that to feel really poised a woman needs not only to look good on the surface, but requires luxury from her skin outwards.'

Vicki was still digesting this, when another thought struck her. 'That woman—Madame Jaubert—I suppose you realise that she thought I was your mistress.'

'Annette? Oh, I am sure you are mistaken,' he replied easily.

'No, I'm not mistaken. And you, of course, did absolutely nothing to dispel her illusion. And that——' she jerked a thumb to the box behind her '—will merely confirm her suspicions.'

'It will not.' His unruffled calmness made her clench her hands savagely in her lap. 'She may wonder, but as I am not in the habit of confiding in my employees——'

Vicki's hands gave a faint, convulsive jerk. 'Your *employees*? You mean you——?'

'But, of course. I own Roxanne—I bought it several years ago.' Did she imagine it, or was there a momentary hardening in his voice? 'I find it useful as an outlet for some of our *prêt-à-porter* clothes. Although small, it has established an excellent reputation and is a valued part of our business, even though most of our fabrics now go direct to a young designer in Paris.'

He flicked a quick glance in her direction. 'You look surprised, *ma petite*. Is the idea of my owning a chic boutique so astonishing?'

'Certainly not,' Vicki snarled. 'Nothing you could ever do would astonish me in the slightest.'

His nod of amused satisfaction merely fuelled her bad temper, but she forced herself to remain silent as he looked past her before swinging out into the busy road which led south towards the mountains.

'As for Annette Jaubert, why should you be in the least concerned for her good opinion?' There was now a razor's edge in his voice. 'After all, you have made it perfectly clear that after your enforced trip to Bordeaux you cannot wait to shake the dust of France from your elegant feet.'

The hotel coffee-shop was almost deserted, most of the guests no doubt, like Gilles, enjoying themselves immensely at the final plenary session of the symposium. He had informed her that she would be bored—as if she needed him to tell her that, she thought, her mind still blown by the day and a half of feverish debate on such earth-shaking matters as the relative merits of soft cream cheese or skimmed milk *fromage frais* in the battle to come to terms with the growing power of the health food lobby. Then he had indulgently said, *'Amuse-toi bien, ma petite.'* So, graciously released from her invisible collar and chain for the afternoon, she had made a second visit to the consulate to collect her temporary passport and had also checked with a travel agent near the hotel that there were seats available on the following day's London flight.

This time tomorrow, she thought with a funny little floorward dip of her stomach, she would be back in her flat, and, she told herself firmly, she could hardly wait. Gilles had been right in that, at least—the sooner she was out of this country and back in familiar surroundings again, the happier she'd be.

And really, she could have left three days ago. What on earth had possessed him to drag her to this wretched conference, anyway? She flicked the spoon against her saucer edgily. She'd done absolutely nothing. True, she'd joined Gilles at some of the small group sessions, trying her best to look intelligent among the welter of meaningless jargon, and he'd also dragged her to the buffet lunch where they'd joined a group of English delegates. But even here Gilles had, of course, done all the talking that really mattered—he had, she reflected moodily, kept his hand very firmly on the tiller, while she must have seemed nothing more than his insignificant little cabin boy.

'So you're playing hookey, too.'

Jerked back from her private thoughts, Vicki looked up at the young man smiling down at her.

'Mind if I join you?' Then, as she hesitated, he indicated the dozen empty tables which surrounded them, 'After all, it's rather crowded in here.'

Well, if it was a pick-up, it was being done in the nicest possible manner, and the young man was very handsome in a fair, boyish way. Come to think of it, he looked rather like Leslie Howard in *Gone With the Wind*... She returned his smile, gesturing him to the chair opposite.

As he slid into it, he held out his hand. 'Mark Thompson.'

'Victoria—Vicki Summers.'

'Ah, thought you were English—I saw you yesterday. How on earth does a girl like you,' momentarily, his eyes slid over her face and her obviously expensive turquoise dress, 'come to be at a do like this?'

Before Vicki could reply, a waiter appeared and set down a tray. They waited until he had gone, then Mark continued, 'Oh, of course.' He was still eyeing her in a speculative way that made her feel rather uncomfortable. 'You're with that Laroque fellow, aren't you? Tell me to mind my own business if you like, but how the hell did you get mixed up with a guy like that?'

'Well,' she began cautiously, 'it's a long story.' Suddenly, she had an almost overwhelming urge to pour out the whole miserable tale to this sympathetic-looking fellow countryman, but pride held her back. 'I'm—I'm returning a favour,' she said at last. 'He helped me out of a tight spot.' And straight into another one, she added as a silent rider.

'I hope you know what you're doing.' He studied her half-averted face thoughtfully. 'From what I've heard, he eats little girls like you for breakfast.'

'And spits out the pips, I suppose.' Behind her weak grin, she felt a momentary stab of guilt at her disloyalty, and suddenly she didn't want to be discussing Gilles, enraging though he was, with this unknown young man. 'Don't worry about me,' she said, in an effort to dismiss this particular topic. 'I'm going back to London tomorrow, just as soon as this thing ends.'

'Oh, great, we can travel together—that's if you're going on the early-morning Air France flight.' He paused for a moment, but when she made no response, he went on casually, 'You work in London?'

'Well, yes and no. I've got nothing definite on at the moment. The job I was hoping to go back to seems to have fallen through so——' she pulled a face '—this time tomorrow I shall no doubt be job-hunting.'

'What do you do?'

'Well, it's PR work I've been doing for Gilles,' she said hesitantly.

'PR, eh? Maybe we can help you, then.'

'We?'

'Yes, my father and I. We're planning a major expansion in the near future—that's why he's sent me to this awful conference—and we could well need someone to take on publicity full-time. We've got an import-export business—delicatessen stuff mainly. That's how I know Laroque. He isn't a real friend of yours, is he?'

'No.' She shook her head warily, wondering what was coming next.

'Well, I'll tell you for free, he's a right bastard to do business with. Mind you, in this trade, they're all bastards. I remember my first solo trip to Germany. Stop me if I'm boring you, by the way.'

Vicki smiled encouragingly. She was beginning to feel as though she'd known Mark for years, so amusing, so easy to talk to.

'. . . and when I got back, Dad said, "Call that a smoked sausage?" and I said . . .'

She was already laughing in anticipation of the punch-line, when the laugh froze on her face. Past Mark's shoulder she could see Gilles, framed in the doorway, watching them. Even at this distance, there was no mistaking the angry frown on his face. As he advanced on them, she was positive that she could feel her insides fluttering in apprehension and then rapidly spiralling downwards towards her new high-heeled shoes.

'Victoria, you are ready? Come.' Totally ignoring Mark, he put a purposeful hand on her chair.

'Well, I——' She swallowed down the nervousness that had been sparked by the anger she could now clearly see in his eyes. This was utterly ridiculous, allowing him to treat her in this way in front of a stranger. But Mark was saving the day for her. Glancing from one to the other, as though to assess the situation, he got to his feet, hand outstretched.

'Laroque. Good to see you again. I was hoping to have a word.'

Gilles, totally ignoring his hand, gave him one swift, annihilating glance which made Vicki cringe, then said dismissively, 'I do not recall our having met, *monsieur*.'

A faint colour tinged Mark's cheeks, but he only said, 'I'm Mark Thompson, of Thompson and Golding. We were interested in doing business with you last year, but——'

'But you were not a large enough enterprise for me to work with,' Gilles cut in brusquely.

Mark, though, was not to be so easily reduced to pulverised dust. 'Ah, but we've expanded greatly since then, Laroque. You really ought to talk to us—me again some time. Perhaps after dinner?'

But Gilles did not respond to him, turning back to Vicki instead. 'You are ready, I trust?'

With great deliberation, she picked up her cup and drained the last lukewarm dregs of coffee, then, reaching for her bag, got slowly to her feet. As she did so, Gilles put his hand firmly on her arm, as though to pre-empt any attempt at flight. He barely acknowledged Mark's, 'Bye, Laroque,' but when Mark called after them, 'Bye, Vicki, see you around—and don't forget my offer,' she felt that hand, for a moment, tighten like steel around her arm.

CHAPTER NINE

ONCE outside, she stopped dead.

'Let go of my arm.' Her voice was very low, but it shook with anger.

His only response was to propel her across the palatial, crowded lobby, a smile of seemingly warm solicitude on his face. Only when they had safely rounded a huge peninsula of potted palms did Vicki, glancing surreptitiously at him, see the synthetic smile fade into those all too familiar hard-planed lines.

He ushered her into one of the lifts and, as the door closed silently on them, jabbed viciously at the button as though venting some of his fury on that innocuous piece of grey plastic.

Outside her room, he held out his hand. 'Your key.'

She fumbled in her bag, feeling the metal cold against her clammy fingers, but trying to delay the moment when they should be in her room. Only when he gave an exclamation of impatience did she draw it out and silently hand it to him.

He closed the door behind them, then leaned against it, his arms folded. Vicki, partly to cover her apprehension and partly to display, however belatedly, some tiny show of spirit, hurled her bag down on to the white, king-sized counterpane and kicked off her shoes, which had been pinching her all afternoon, sending one in a vicious spiral to narrowly miss Gilles' head before thumping against the door.

She turned her back on him and walked across the room, the sound of her feet lost in the deep-piled white carpet, and gazed fixedly out of the window, studying the magnificent view above the rooftops to the River Garonne, flowing swiftly through the very centre of the city. Her arm was sore, and when she glanced down she saw, across the creamy flesh, the distinct impressions of Gilles' fingers, already a dull bluish tinge.

'What were you doing?'

His voice had an arctic chill in it, and when she turned to look at him in total incomprehension he added, 'Downstairs—in the coffee-shop, with that so-charming young man.'

What on earth had got into him this time? Had Mark unwittingly fallen so foul of him at their previous meeting that Gilles was now reacting in this utterly boorish way? But no, in their brief acquaintance she had already registered that, however unreasonably he might behave towards her, his attitude towards everyone else—from his beloved sheep upwards—was unfailingly courteous and correct or, at least, had been until now. And so—she swallowed hard against the tight little lump of fear—yet again she must be the target of his unreasoning anger. But she must not give him the satisfaction of seeing her apprehension.

'You dragged me here to speak to Englishmen—remember?' she snapped. 'Well, I was.'

'Yes, but I did not tell you to leap at the first one you encountered.'

'I did not,' she said between clenched teeth, 'leap at him.'

'No?' he enquired with savagely polite irony. 'I certainly seemed to interrupt an intimate little tête-à-tête when I arrived.'

'Oh, don't be so ridiculous. We——'

'What precisely did he mean—don't forget my offer?'

'That's absolutely no concern of yours,' she flared. 'You're not my keeper—not any longer. I'm organising my own life from now on, without any interference from anyone, particularly an arrogant, overbearing——'

But then, catching sight of them both in the wide-angled dressing-table mirror, she stopped abruptly. They were glowering at each other, for all the world like a pair of prize-fighters, sizing each other up for a life or death struggle. She had to defuse this, before the electric sparks in the air between them blew a fuse and burst into uncontrollable flame.

'Look, Gilles,' she went on, in a slightly steadier tone, 'let's stop this. I'm leaving tomorrow——'

'There is no need for you to leave tomorrow.'

'Yes, Gilles, there is—*every need*.' She put as much emphasis on the words as she could. 'The conference is over, and so there's nothing—absolutely nothing—to keep me in France any longer.' She paused to try and gauge the effect she was having, but Gilles' expression was now completely impassive, so she went on, 'If you must know, Mark was telling me about a job he might be able to find for me in London, and,' she grimaced, 'as you've gathered, I'll be glad of any work that's offered. I've checked and there's a flight at lunchtime that I can get—so can't we part, if not friends,' she gave him a rueful smile, 'at least in a civilised manner?'

Gilles was silent for a moment, as though assimilating her words, but then, to her intense relief, his face relaxed. 'Yes, you are right, Victoria. *When* we part, it will be far better for us to remain—friends.'

He smiled faintly at her, but even as Vicki released an inward sigh of relief a prickle of unease ran up her spine. She didn't quite like the emphasis he'd placed on that 'when'. He couldn't be planning some new device to hold her here even longer, could he? Of course not. He would be as pleased to be relieved of his temporary captive as she would be to be free of him. And yet—past events had shown her all too clearly that, however much he might appear to accept defeat in any battle of wills between them, that acquiescence merely masked a redoubled determination to emerge the victor.

That slight smile was still there as he continued, 'And so, I shall leave you now to prepare for dinner. *A bientôt*.' And he was gone.

Vicki sank down on to the bed, listening to his key turn in the lock of the next room, the door open then close again. She stared at the rose-patterned wall so hard that it almost seemed to dissolve to enable her to see Gilles, but then, after a few minutes, she roused herself and went through to the luxurious bathroom to shampoo her hair.

When she had finished, she set the bath water running slowly and sat at the dressing-table to dry her hair. She moved the dryer mechanically about her head while she studied her reflection dispassionately, as though the face belonged to someone she'd never met before.

She remembered, too late, that she'd intended asking Gilles for a 'loan' to buy some make-up in the hotel boutique, but maybe it didn't matter. Those alarming hollows had now filled out—all that Laroque cheese, she thought ironically—and the dark, haunted shadows brushed beneath her wide-set grey eyes had all but gone too, while all that mountain air had given her the light but becoming tan which, with her creamy skin, was all she ever managed.

Gilles had said she was beautiful when she laughed... Tentatively she smiled at herself, then at the infectious grin in the mirror, her cheeks flushed and she shook her gleaming chestnut hair back so that it bounced against her face. She switched off the dryer, then, hearing her bath water, fled just in time to prevent a catastrophe.

Afterwards, half dried and wrapped in the enormous lemon bathsheet, she returned to the bedroom. The previous evening, partly from the fatigue of an over-full day, partly from a desire to show her independence, she had not bothered to change and had gone to dinner wearing the apricot dress minus its jacket.

It hung on the rail now, but beside it was that black sliver of a dress which had so excitingly, so disturbingly clung to her body in the changing room of Roxanne. Eight hundred pounds worth of Laroque fabric! She had already made up her mind to parcel it up unworn and send it back to the shop via its rightful owner. But all at once sinful temptation wriggled its insidious way into her mind, all her willpower buckling feebly before it. After all, it *was* the last night... Somehow, she wasn't sure from where, she would find the money to pay Gilles for this dress as well as the other two—she must wear it this evening.

She lifted it down and laid it on the bed. Absently, she finished drying herself and tossed the bathsheet on to a chair, before taking from a drawer some of the underwear which Monique had brought for her. Then she stopped, a faint frown on her face. The bra would show; even without trying the dress on again, she remembered how those little crescents of white cotton had revealed themselves each time she'd moved. On the other hand, the dress was so—*slight* that there was simply no way that she was going to eat dinner with Gilles sitting opposite her without wearing something underneath it.

Her eyes strayed to the bottom of the wardrobe... That black and gold box, which she'd thrust into the lowest drawer of her dressing-table the moment they'd returned from Toulouse and that she had fondly imagined still languished there, until that knock at the door last evening and Gilles' soft purr: 'I think you inadvertently forgot these when you were packing.' She had opened the door and snatched up the box, absolutely determined not even to look at its contents, let alone wear them, but tonight...

She took up the box and placed it beside the dress. Her fingers trembling slightly, she slowly raised the lid and there lay the beautiful silk lingerie, gleaming with pearly lustre in the early evening light. Hardly aware of what she was doing, she lifted out the ivory bra. Beneath it was a tiny wisp of matching panties, below that another set in creamy coffee. Then she drew out, with a faint sibilant hiss of reverence, a full-length nightdress of silver-grey silk, surely too lovely ever to be worn merely in the bedroom, she mused, and yet, as she held its cool folds of nothingness against her naked body, certainly too revealing ever to be worn outside it.

Wonderingly, she surveyed herself in the mirror, the grey silk reflecting off her eyes to give them a strange, almost unearthly sheen, as though she were being transformed into a silver-eyed pagan goddess. Hardly breathing, she stared at herself for a few moments, then an expression almost like fear crossed her face and next moment she had snatched the nightdress away and thrown it back on to the bed.

She slipped on the ivory bra and pants, this time not allowing herself to gaze at her reflection, then picked up the black dress. It slid down over her breasts and hips, caressing her with its softness. She smoothed it down and, her fingers stiff and clumsy, she tore out the pins which had secured her hair during her bath and dragged the comb through it. Then she paused, the words of the woman in Roxanne flashing unbidden into her mind, and she piled her hair up into a huge knot on her nape.

Only when she had finished did she look at herself. The dress was beautiful, its chic simplicity perfectly setting off the lines of her slim body. And tonight *she* was beautiful too, she realised, though with that same irrational flicker of fear. Her cheeks were still flushed, her eyes huge still, with that shimmer of grey, and now with a hint of wildness in them, while her body seemed to be held, lightly poised, as though an electric tension was running through every limb to her nerve-ends.

She picked up her bag, then stood, her hand on the doorknob while she drew in a deep, steadying breath, released the breath slowly and felt a little of the tension drain away.

There was, as she had half expected, no answer when she tentatively knocked at Gilles' door. He was in the foyer, talking to a group of men, dressed like him in immaculately cut dark grey suits. He saw her at once though, broke off what he was saying and began threading his way through the crowd.

Vicki stood quite still, almost unconscious now of the people, the subdued chatter, the lights—of everything except Gilles. She watched him coming towards her, his eyes holding hers all the time. When he reached her, he did not at first say anything, only stood looking at her.

'I—I'm sorry I'm late.' Her voice was husky.

He was still regarding her unsmilingly, his eyes black against the light, the veiled expression in them unreadable, though something about his silence tightened her already taut nerves another notch, that same fear which she had experienced up in her room flickering about in her mind like summer lightning.

She took a step backwards, coming up against the rasping fronds of a palm, and put her hand up almost as though to ward him off. But he took her hand, his grip tightening on it as she tried to pull away, and carried it to his lips in a formal kiss.

Behind them, an elderly couple emerged from one of the lifts and passed them, taking in with avid curiosity the interesting cameo scene which was being enacted.

Vicki jerked her hand away in confusion. 'You're very French—very Gallic tonight.'

But her attempt at a bantering remark did nothing to break the spell that held them. He straightened up, with the merest hint of a smile.

'But *chérie*...' his voice lingered on the word in a way which made her breathing, already shallow, become even more hurried '...you forget, I *am* French—Gallic. And when I see such a lovely young woman—her loveliness enhanced by a Laroque creation—well——'

The old, familiar mockery, the ironic gleam in his eye, were back. She knew instinctively that he was doing it deliberately, setting her free from that spell, and at once she felt more comfortable, marginally more confident of her ability to handle the evening now that the enigmatic, almost brooding look had gone from his eyes.

Settling his arm lightly around her waist, he guided her towards the restaurant. Inside, although the room was large, the pretty white trellis divisions between each candlelit table gave it a cosy intimacy.

The *maître d'* was leading them through the room when, out of the corner of her eye, Vicki caught sight of Mark. He was staring at her in rapt, almost open-mouthed astonishment and she could not resist a private little glow of pleasure at the effect her appearance was so clearly producing. He and another man were sitting at a table for four, and when he caught her eye he gestured invitingly in the direction of the two empty places. Both she and the *maître d'* hesitated, but next moment a hand was giving her a firm push in the small of her back and they were past and heading for a small table beside the long floor-length windows which gave on to the terrace.

A waiter appeared and handed her a gilt-embossed menu. She opted for the *'potage crème de champignons'*, then, peering anxiously at the elegant, hand-written curlicues, finally located the three vegetarian main dishes tucked away at the bottom.

The wine waiter was hovering and Gilles, after casting a swift, practised eye down the list, looked at her enquiringly. 'What are you eating?'

'The *roulade* of spinach,' she said firmly.

'Mon Dieu!' Gilles rolled his eyes in mock despair. 'When you have such riches to choose from. And what wine, I wonder, is best suited to accompany such a dish?' He turned back to the waiter, who seemed almost as upset as himself, and shrugged resignedly. 'A magnum of Dom Perignon, I think.'

The *roulade* was superb, light and melting, the mound of delicately butter-sautéd fresh vegetables which accompanied it equally delicious. Vicki laid down her knife and fork, leaned back and dabbed her mouth. 'Mmm, that was wonderful.'

Beside her, through the windows, she could see the gardens. By daylight, though beautifully tended, they were mundane enough, but now, softly floodlit, and with a fountain which alternately leapt and fell, an unearthly blue-green plume of water, they had a magical quality. Perhaps after dinner they could stroll out there. Last night, after their meal, Gilles had suggested that they should go outside for a while, but she, feeling a sudden reluctance to be with him in such a potentially intimate setting, had pleaded fatigue and retreated to her room.

Tonight, though, it would be rather pleasant and, after all it was their last evening together. Their last evening . . . This time tomorrow she'd be hundreds of miles from here, hundreds of miles from Gilles, and it would not merely be the English Channel which would stretch as an unbridgeable gulf between them . . .

At his elbow was the by now half-empty magnum of champagne, set in a silver ice-bucket, the metal frosting over in the warmth of the room. She took a sip from her glass, then held it in front of her, watching the single thread of bubbles make its lazy way to the surface where it broke with a soundless plop.

Gilles had said that the very best champagne did not burst in an explosion of bubbles 'like health salts', as he had put it, with an expression of acute distaste. It didn't really matter, of course—she wasn't going to be drinking nectar like this again in a hurry—but still, it was nice to know these things.

Gilles glanced up, and as he met her eye he smiled at her. All the harshness, all the hard lines, had faded from his face; for once, he had lost that taut, tightly coiled quality. The blue eyes, so often cold and unyielding, had a warmth she had never seen before. His tanned face, set into sharp relief by the white expanse of shirt . . . How handsome he was . . . A faintly painful sensation stirred in her, almost like regret. If things had been different between them . . .

The waiter returned, bearing an enormous cheeseboard. She carefully focused on it, then gave him a dazzling smile. 'I would like some Laroque, please.'

The man hesitated, then pointed with the knife to a hunk of pale gold cheese. 'We have Pyrenéan, but I regret that we do not have Laroque. Perhaps *mademoiselle* would care to try this one.'

But when she crumbled the tiny piece and tasted it, she said firmly, 'No, this is not the same at all.'

She stopped, shaking her head slightly to clear it from the blanket of woolliness which seemed to be rapidly smothering her brain. 'Laroque cheese,' she continued, enunciating each word with great care, 'is much nicer than this.'

Over her head, she sensed Gilles and the waiter exchange glances, then Gilles, his eyes dancing with barely suppressed laughter, put a hand over hers.

'This one is excellent.' He pointed to a pale, creamy-looking cheese. '*Mademoiselle* will have some of that—and that.'

As the waiter was serving her, he leaned down towards her and said confidingly, 'I promise that next time *mademoiselle* dines here, there will be Laroque Pyrenéan for her.'

Next time—but there would never be a next time! Vicki bit her lip and blinked away the slightly maudlin tears that suddenly filled her eyes. Fortunately, Gilles did not appear to have noticed, for he sat back in his chair, regarding her with a broad grin.

'I don't see what's so funny,' she said coldly, and spread a piece of the creamy cheese very neatly on to two water biscuits.

His face instantly became deadpan. 'You are right—there is nothing funny at all. I was merely thinking what an unrecognised asset I have had lurking under my roof all this time. I believe that if I took you on a tour of the best hotels in France, at the end of a month every one of them would be telephoning me, begging for a supply of our cheese. Of course,' he added thoughtfully, though with a swift, wicked glance at her, 'it might prove to be rather heavy on champagne.'

He lifted the bottle and leaned across to refill her glass, but she put out her hand. 'No more for me, thank you. I've had enough.'

But he filled her glass a quarter full, then poured the last of the wine into his. He lifted his glass and held it towards her.

'A toast, Victoria, to you. May you gain your heart's desire—whatever that may be.'

There was no smile now, and even as she raised her glass to his she was aware of an indefinable undercurrent in his voice. She murmured, 'And to you, Gilles; may——' then broke off, quite unable to return his toast.

He nodded acknowledgment, however, then drained his glass, but Vicki sat, staring at him, her glass still suspended. 'Your heart's desire.' Just what was her heart's desire? And then, with sudden, dazzling clarity, she knew. It was to be with this man, sitting opposite her, remain with him forever. But tomorrow morning he was going to drive her to the airport and then she would never see him again... It couldn't be—she couldn't possibly... She didn't even like him—so arrogant, so calculating—and yet that, she knew, had absolutely nothing to do with it. Her foolish, treacherous heart had betrayed her...

She raised her glass to her lips with unsteady hands and gulped the wine without tasting it, but as she put it down she met Gilles' eye. He had been watching her, his face now wholly serious, and he put his hand over hers.

'Victoria——'

'Laroque! Gilles Laroque.'

Vicki's head jerked round. A thick-set man with a florid complexion was standing over them, and she felt Gilles' hand stiffen as he glanced up.

He nodded briefly. 'Brague.' His tone was curt, but the man ignored the unwelcoming chill in his voice and put out his hand, which Gilles barely touched in the briefest of greetings.

'How are you, old boy? I didn't expect to see you here—good lord, it must be really something to tempt you down out of your mountain stronghold. It's been a long time, a very long time...' His voice was lachrymose, his heavy face flushed an unpleasant dusky red.

'Yes, it has. And now, if you'll excuse us——'

For apparently the first time the man's eyes registered Vicki. Ignoring Gilles' unsubtle hint, he seized her hand before she could draw back and, in a travesty of that kiss which Gilles had given her, planted his soft, fleshy lips on it.

He straightened up, breathing an acrid gust of cigar and brandy fumes directly into her face, and peered down at her through the flickering candlelight. 'My dear Claudia, as charming and beautiful as ever.' His all-embracing look was that of the practised roué, and made her feel as though he had publicly torn the flimsy black dress from her. 'Now you two must join me for a cognac—I insist.'

'No.' Gilles' voice was, if possible, even more forbidding.

'But my dear boy,' he protested, his voice rising, 'I haven't seen you for years, and as for Claudia——'

Vicki closed her eyes for a moment. This was horrible. Silence was falling throughout the restaurant, conversations suspended, while people at the neighbouring tables were watching covertly. Two waiters were hovering, as though they might be needed.

'This is not Claudia.' Gilles' level voice crackled with ice.

The stranger stared stupidly, first at him, then at her. 'Oh, *mademoiselle*, a thousand apologies. Not Claudia, no, of course not. I see that now.' He leered salaciously down at Vicki so that her skin crawled, then gave Gilles a sly, knowing wink. 'I'll say this for you, old man, you certainly know how to pick them.'

He put his hand on her upper arm, his pudgy fingers pawing her flesh, brushing as though by accident against her breast, until, almost beside herself, she gave a half-suppressed cry and cringed away from him. Gilles leapt to his feet with an exclamation of anger, put his hands squarely on the man's chest and pushed him off his feet and back into the chair he had just vacated, where he sat gaping up at them like a stranded goldfish.

Gilles turned to her. 'Come.'

His voice was brusque and, ignoring the waiter who had leapt forward, he drew back her chair. As she got rather unsteadily to her feet he seemed to hesitate, then, surprisingly, he rested his hand gently for a moment on the man's shoulder.

In the doorway, she could not prevent herself glancing round. A waiter was bending over the man, but he still sat where Gilles had left him, staring after them, his brandy-glass half lifted to his lips.

CHAPTER TEN

HARDLY aware of Gilles beside her, Vicki leaned against a pillar, then straightened up immediately as she caught the enquiring looks of the two receptionists at the far end of the foyer. She felt soiled, contaminated by the sordid little scene, and when he took her arm she shook him off.

'Don't touch me!'

'Not here, I beg you.'

His voice was under ruthless control, but when, for the first time, she brought herself to look directly at him, she saw that he was very pale, his face set once again in harsh-etched lines. Clearly, that squalid encounter had also shaken him—and far more than he was prepared to admit.

'You need a drink——' he began, but she shook her head violently. Go into the bar, where some of those avid spectators would no doubt soon follow, alight with curiosity to view the next act of the drama?

'No—no, thank you,' she said, her mouth stiff. 'I don't want anything.'

Gilles scanned the expanse of lobby, the huge gilt rococo mirrors, then drew her behind the pillar so that they were partly screened. 'We will go into the garden, then.'

He took her arm, but, feeling her tense away from him once more, he loosed his hold, his mouth tightening. She sagged back against the pillar, feeling the marble chill strike through her dress. A sick lethargy, brought on, she supposed dispassionately, by the shock that had so crudely shattered that mood of champagne-induced euphoria, was oozing like sludge through her entire body. The only thing she wanted now was to be alone, to shut out the whole world, and most of all Gilles. Somehow, she had to get rid of Gilles.

'You go and have a drink,' she said abruptly, then added, with the pallid ghost of a smile, 'You look as though you could do with one. I'm going up to my room. Goodnight.'

But even as she went to walk past him he caught her wrist and whirled her round to face him. At that same moment the restaurant doors opened and two couples emerged, laughing uproariously. The laughs died on the instant that they saw them, and Vicki, all her senses flayed, felt them almost tiptoe past, before thc laughter, now discreetly subdued, began again. She felt sick to her stomach.

Gilles, his face dark with anger, swore violently and slammed his fist against the pillar, then, towing her behind him strode across to the lifts and almost pushed her inside one.

Once at her door, she opened it slightly and tried to slip in, but he was too quick for her. Putting his hand on it, he thrust it wide open, so that it banged against the wall, and followed her in. The room was in darkness, apart from a shaft of blue-green light from the floodlit gardens below which lit their strained faces, transforming them into weird subterranean creatures. Gilles flicked the switch and the eerie underwater sensation disappeared in the gentle rose-glow of the wall lights.

With exaggerated care, she laid her bag on the dressing-table, and, ignoring him completely, went through to the bathroom. She closed the door and leaned against it, then very slowly she went over to the washbasin and turned the tap on with a violent jerk. She stood for a long time, idly watching the jet of cold water play over her hands and wrists, only stopping when the veins contracted painfully with the icy chill. She caught up handfuls of water and splashed them over her face again and again, until her whole mind was numbed with the cold.

As she dried herself, her eyes looked back at her from the mirror, wide and staring—exactly like that wild creature which Gilles had compared her with. And yet that scene downstairs, unpleasant though it was, had surely been nothing more than a brief brush with a man too drunk to know what he was doing, a man she would never set eyes on again. It certainly hadn't been enough to cause a reaction of such violence in her.

In the middle of replacing the towel with mathematical precision on the rail, she stopped dead. What a self-deluding fool she'd been, to allow herself to believe for an instant that a stranger's alcoholic kiss, even his eyes lasciviously stripping her, could have torn away her composure so completely.

Months before, wounded and bleeding, though the hurt had been all within her, she had like a hermit crab taken refuge in a hard protective shell which she had painfully constructed around herself. She had done it over months of private anguish until she had believed that she was inviolate, no chink of weakness left in her. Now, in a moment, that careful protective layer had been brutally ripped away, and all the feelings she had believed subdued forever raged once more within her.

She was jealous—jealous of all the women whom that man Brague had encompassed in that knowing wink, that salacious leer... *'I'll say this for you, old man, you certainly know how to pick them...'* And above all, she knew with searing self-understanding, she was jealous of this unknown woman, this Claudia.

A despairing groan burst from her. Oh, if only Gilles had let her go when she'd finished the brochure. Perhaps, subconsciously, she'd known even then that her feelings for him had irrevocably changed from the fear and hatred of the captive for her captor to another, much more subversive and destructive emotion. If she'd left even two days before, she might never have divined the truth, and, once she was safely back in London it might have quietly faded away to nothing...

But now Gilles was in the next room—and everything was different.

She went back into the bedroom. He was at the open window, his back to her. His jacket lay on the bed in a crumpled heap; mechanically she picked it up and draped it over the back of a chair, then retrieved his silver-grey tie which had slipped on to the floor.

'I'm sorry.' He did not turn.

'Oh.' She gave an infinitesimal shrug. 'Don't worry. I've got over it now.' She stopped, then driven by some inner compulsion, went on, her voice almost cracking with the effort to appear casual, 'By the way, who's Claudia? Or shouldn't I ask?'

'My——' there was a long pause '—wife.'

'Your *wife*?'

'Yes.' He slowly turned to her now, a weariness in his face that she had never seen before. 'Tonight was not wholly Brague's fault—apart, that is, from the fact that he is a drunken sot. You have a remarkable resemblance to Claudia—slim, with chestnut hair—except,' he gave her a brief smile with no hint of amusement in it, 'that you have a softness, a vulnerability which I would guess she lacked from the age of three.'

As though unable to keep still any longer, he began to prowl around the room, Vicki watching him in silence. He sat down heavily on the bed, hunching forward with his elbows resting on his knees.

'I met her in Paris—she managed one of the expensive boutiques on the Rive Gauche. She was beautiful, with a kind of hectic gaiety, and I'd never met a woman like her.'

The utter bleakness in his voice pierced Vicki to the heart. Scarcely aware of what she was doing, she sat beside him and took his large hand between hers.

'Please don't, Gilles—it's too painful for you. Don't go on.'

But he continued, almost as though he were talking to himself, his voice raw. 'We married, but within months it had all gone wrong. Claudia was a Parisienne born and bred, and she quickly grew to hate the valley—my valley. She hated its isolation, its remoteness, and above all she hated the mountains.' He gave her a frayed smile. 'She was rather like you in that also. I bought the shop—Roxanne—for her, but it was no use. All that we shared was a physical passion for each other, but there was nothing else, and after a year she left without a word and returned to Paris. Only afterwards did I learn that she had discovered she was pregnant,' his tight voice shook slightly, 'and had got rid of the baby—*our* child—as quickly as she could.'

'Oh, no.' Vicki put a hand to her mouth. 'Gilles, I'm so sorry.'

Beside this stark tragedy, her own unhappiness, sparked by the episode in the restaurant, now seemed trivial. Hardly aware of what she was doing, possessed only by the desperate need to give comfort to this proud, hard man, she reached out and pulled him to her, her arms going round him to cradle him against her.

He tensed, as though to thrust her away, but then his taut body relaxed. Her cheek against his hair, she whispered, 'And she's still in Paris, or—or has she remarried?'

She faltered on the last words, but there was no prurient curiosity in her question. She knew, with sudden perceptive clarity, that Gilles' pride had never before allowed him to unburden so much of himself as he was doing now. And she also knew that he must finish the story, for not until then could he begin to purge himself of it.

'No. She is dead.' His voice was strangely quiet as he spoke the shocking word. 'Although I was unaware of it, long before we were married she had been regularly taking amphetamines.' Vicki's arms closed convulsively on him for a moment. 'Once she was back in Paris, one of her—boyfriends introduced her to hard drugs. I paid for several courses of treatment for her in a private clinic in Switzerland, but it was useless. She died a year ago.'

Vicki closed her eyes. There was nothing to say. Drugs—of course. That explained everything: why he'd reacted with such violence at the *auberge* that morning, why he'd been so harsh, his contemptuous hostility towards her so barely suppressed.

She was never sure how long they sat there, perfectly motionless, until outside in the corridor the lift disgorged some guests, and they walked past, chatting animatedly, one of them brushing against the door. Gilles stirred and drew away from her. He straightened up and regarded her, a tiny smile softening the bleakness of his face.

'Thank you.'

'For what?'

'For listening.'

There was something in his dark eyes which made her abruptly drop her own. For the first time she became uncomfortably aware of how close they were sitting: his knee and the hard line of his thigh were against hers. She wanted to edge away but dared not move even an inch, so instead began fidgeting with the rumpled counterpane, picking nervously at the fluffy white candlewick.

'Vicki.'

Her hand closed convulsively on the fabric, totally thrown off balance, more by the gentleness—no, tenderness in his voice than by this, his first use of her pet name, and before she could recollect the folly of such an action her eyes had jerked to his face.

Hardly seeming to breathe, they stared into one another's eyes, hungrily, as though to devour what they saw there, for what seemed an endless time. Then they were reaching towards each other, tentatively, as though in slow motion. Only when their fingers touched did Gilles' hands lock on to hers.

He snatched her into his arms, smothering her face, her neck and the top of her breasts with ravening kisses, while Vicki, her eyes closing under the ecstasy of his touch, the sensual drag of his skin across hers, yielded fluidly to his embrace, her own arms straining him to her. When he eased his body away from hers for a moment, she gave a little moan and tried to hold him to her.

'Sssh,' he whispered against her throat, then his hands were on the zip of her dress, first fumbling at the top, then roughly tearing it apart so that she felt it give all the way down to the small of her back, the delicate fabric ripping under his hands. With one arm he raised her up into his arms, pulling the ruined dress from her and throwing it on to the floor.

She lay passive in his arms, feeling his fingers release the tiny hook of her bra, then they were sliding down each side of her body to draw the flimsy silk panties from over her hips. He laid her down, then he too was naked. As she opened her arms he came down into them, pressing her into the bed under the urgent demand of his body.

He slipped one arm behind her, resting it for a moment against the soft mounds of her buttocks before raising her to meet him. She tensed, then a shuddering, half-stifled cry was ripped from her as a spear thrust of pain tore into her very softness.

The next instant, Gilles lay frozen in her arms, his breathing harsh and uneven, and then he withdrew himself from her. She lay, her eyes tightly shut, feeling him sit back on his haunches beside her. He drew in a deep, ragged breath, the sound frighteningly loud in the silent room.

'Why did you lie to me?'

When she did not answer, he grabbed her by the shoulders, dragging her upright, her head hanging forward, screened by her fall of hair. He seized a handful and pulled her head up so that she was forced to meet his eyes, glinting now not with desire, but fierce anger.

'Why did you lie to me?' he repeated, jerking her savagely as he spoke. 'Your being married, your husband—it was all lies, wasn't it?'

When she tried to shake her head in denial, his fingers tightened on her hair so that tears sprang to her eyes. 'Wasn't it? Did you think that I really would not be aware that you are—*were*,' his lips twisted in a spasm, 'a virgin?' He almost spat out the word, as though it were a term of abuse—which perhaps it was, in his vocabulary. 'One does not make love to a young, virginal girl in the same way as one does to an experienced woman.'

Her face felt tight and awkward, as if it had been assembled from a kit of several sets of ill-matched features. Somehow, though, she forced herself to meet his sapphire gaze, and somehow she found her voice.

'I didn't lie to you, Gilles,' she said very quietly. 'I told you the truth, I swear it—yes!' as he went to interrupt. 'It's just that I didn't tell you the whole truth. I *was* married, and David *did* go off with someone else.' She gave him a small, brittle smile, then looked away. 'The only thing I didn't tell you was that he went off with a man.'

She hardly heard his shocked intake of breath but hurried on, her voice jerky, 'He should never have got married, of course. It was his mother. She was an elderly, rich widow... She always terrified me, and I think she terrified her only son as well. She must have suspected—she threatened to leave all her money to a distant cousin of his if he didn't marry. I didn't know that until afterwards, but I don't blame him—not for that. He'd been spoilt, given everything he wanted, and he could never have managed on his lecturer's salary. A month after she died, he left me.'

All the heart-rending desolation was flooding back, threatening to overwhelm her, to bring on again the breakdown she had suffered months before. But she drove herself on. 'It—it was quite easy to get a divorce.'

Gilles went to put his arms round her but, desperately afraid that in his arms the last shreds of her composure would shatter like fragile crystal, she pushed him away, curling into herself instead, hugging her arms to comfort herself as she went on, her voice wooden, 'We never made love. At first he made excuses, then he blamed me—said it was all my fault, that I was frigid, that I didn't turn him on.'

'Oh, mon Dieu!' Ignoring her frantic struggles, Gilles caught hold of her again, and this time pulled her close against him, into the shelter of his arms. '*Bâtard*—if I could get my hands on him, for what he's done to you!'

This was what she'd dreaded, what her mind had cringed from—the questions, the anger.

'No, don't say that! It's——' she began, then stopped. She was going to say, It doesn't matter, it's all over. But then, quite suddenly, she began to cry. She bit the back of her hand in a desperate effort to hold back the tears, but they leapt scalding hot from her eyes, spilling on to her cheeks and over her hand.

A gentle, inexorable grip was drawing her hand away from her mouth, the teeth-marks white against the already purpling flesh. She had all but forgotten Gilles—he was only a pair of strong, sheltering arms, but then, 'If you want to bite someone, bite me,' he whispered against her hair, and with an incoherent sound, half-sob, half-laugh, she turned her head against his chest, to weep out all her misery, all her despair, as he gently rocked her shaking body.

When at last the racking sobs had died into an occasional quiver, he caught up the soft counterpane and mopped her swollen face. He held his hand against her cheek for a moment, in a tender, almost maternal caress, which made her want to cry again, then, 'Did I hurt you very much, *mon petit agneau*—my little lamb?'

'What?' The sharp physical pain of her violation had become engulfed in the far greater mental anguish. 'Oh, no, n-not really.'

'I was a brute, an unfeeling, insensitive brute.'

His voice was rough, his face ravaged with self-disgust, and she said quickly, 'But you didn't know. How could you?'

He shook his head, impatient of her understanding. 'I should have guessed. There was always some quality about you, an untouched innocence, like that young girl with the unicorn, as pure as the flowers at her feet, and I——' his lips tightened '—I have deflowered that innocence forever.'

He straightened up, dragged on his shirt and trousers, then stood looking down at her, his eyes sombre, a faint frown creasing his brow.

'Are you still in pain?' His voice was remote, as if he were a doctor, called to the bedside of a patient. 'Shall I run a bath for you?'

What was he saying? She shivered, then stared up at him stupidly. He still didn't really understand. Though her body still throbbed, it wasn't the physical pain, it was the mental trauma of the past years, now so rawly exposed, that was making her react like this.

'I——' she began, then stopped. Gilles was bending towards her. She felt him put his hand on her shoulder; he said something under his breath, then sat her up, his hands under her elbows, supporting her as though she were a broken-stringed puppet.

He picked up the grey silk nightdress, hesitated, then dropped it and took up the white cotton one which the maid had left folded on her pillow that morning. He slid it down over her, carefully lifting her heavy hair out of the way, then scooped her up into his arms like a child. But surely they'd played that scene before, somewhere; she in her cotton nightie, in his arms, his face set, just as it was now?

'Don't be angry,' she tried to say, but her tongue was glued to the roof of her mouth.

He lifted the bedclothes back, then laid her down, her head sinking on to the pillow. He drew up the sheet again, and a moment later she heard his voice on the room telephone. He switched off all but one light, and through half-closed eyes she saw him go and stand by the window, looking out, his back to her until, what was surely only seconds later, there was a soft knock at the door. The door opened, then closed, and Gilles slipped a hot-water bottle down beside her.

There was a clink of glass, then he was hoisting her upright once more, holding a beaker to her lips. 'You must drink some of this.'

Obediently she took a sip, then jerked her head away. 'Ugh, horrible!'

'Drink it, Vicki. It's hot milk with a little cognac—it will help you to sleep. *Yes*,' as she protested feebly.

When she had drained the beaker, he laid her back down. He switched off the final light so that the room took on that faint, blue-green glow again, and put his hand lightly on her forehead. 'Goodnight.'

She clutched at it beseechingly. 'Don't leave me, *please*.'

As soon as he went, all the formless monsters that inhabited the innermost recesses of her mind were sure to come crawling out yet again, writhing around the dark corners of the room like terrifying spectres of the past.

He hesitated, then squeezed her hand. 'Of course I shall stay, all night if you wish.'

He slipped out of his shoes and trousers, drew back the bedclothes, and slid in beside her. Gently, he turned her to him. How safe she felt in his arms, so warm and secure.

'Mmm, you feel just like James,' she murmured.

'James?' There was the very faintest edge to his voice.

'My giant teddy bear.' It was a sleepy mumble.

'Oh.'

She felt him laugh silently against her, then he began softly stroking her hair. In the darkness, she smiled, closed her eyes and drifted off to sleep, still smiling...

She woke with a start, as though something had disturbed her. She yawned, stretched and rolled over, the previous night temporarily forgotten, but then, catching sight of the expanse of rumpled bed beside her, she sat bolt upright, her heart thumping.

On the pillow was the indentation where Gilles' head had rested. She picked it up and smelled the faintest aroma of him; when she rested her cheek against it, she felt the last lingering warmth of his body. So he had stayed with her, as he had promised, the whole night.

She dropped the pillow hastily and lay back again, pulling the sheet up to her chin as though he might materialise on the instant from her silent bathroom. Clutching the sheet, she stared up at the ceiling. What a fool she'd been. How could she have let it happen? She could have insisted on coming up to her room alone, have made Gilles leave her in the lobby or outside her door. But then she gave a wry smile. Made him? No one made Gilles do anything he didn't want to do.

Now he knew everything about her, more than any other human being. He'd stripped her, not only bodily—she went scarlet at the memory—but mentally as well. Gilles had, of course, also revealed himself to her: the unexpected encounter with Brague had forced from him those revelations of his own unhappiness, but, whereas he had shown himself strong enough to accept her sympathy, she could not in her turn bear to receive his pity.

She had anticipated his anger—had perhaps even prepared herself subconsciously for it—but what she couldn't stand was his compassion. What had he called her—'*mon petit agneau*, my little lamb'? Last night, he'd cared for her, comforted her, his strong hands tending her as though she were a forlorn, bedraggled little lamb, and now, her trampled pride still raw and smarting, she simply could not bear to see again that look, not of love, but of pity in his eyes.

Too restless now to stay in bed, she pushed back the sheet, then swung her feet to the floor. As she went to stand up, her eyes fell on the tray on her bedside-table, the empty brandy-glass still on it. Even as she shuddered in revulsion at the remembered taste, she saw, propped up against the glass, a folded piece of the cream hotel writing paper.

She opened it slowly, and saw Gilles' hasty scrawl. He must have sat over there at the dressing-table, writing very quietly, so as not to disturb her. She carried the paper over to the window; it was still early, the rays of the sun turning the rooftops a muted gold.

Leaning against the frame, she read.

> Vicki, I have an appointment for a working breakfast with some Italian businessmen. I have given orders that you are not to be disturbed, but room service will bring you breakfast when you ring for it. I shall be back very soon, when we must talk. G.

She read it through twice, very slowly, then, her eyes smarting, she crumpled it in her hands. 'We must talk.' Talk? What was there to talk about? She'd said everything she was going to say, had revealed everything she would ever reveal. And she forced herself to accept the cold-light-of-the day truth: there was no word of love in the brief, almost curt note. Gilles had never spoken one word of love to her, not even last night, so what more was there for either of them to say?

And then another thought struck her. He'd said, yesterday, that there was no need for her to leave today. Now he might try to persuade her to stay with him—not only out of compassion, but also through some misplaced feelings of guilt, perhaps—to return with him to the valley. But suddenly the thought of going back there, to those mountains whose outstretched arms, from that very first day, had seemed to hold, not the promise of an embrace but the threat of a trap poised ready to spring, leapt vividly into her mind. She had to get away before he came back!

Get away? She'd tried, so feebly, so ineffectually, to escape from him twice before, but now she wasn't marooned in Gilles' isolated valley—she was just a short taxi ride from Bordeaux airport. Even as the thought flared in her mind, she remembered Mark's words... 'the early-morning Air France flight'...

Think! She must think. What time was it now? Outside, the light was growing stronger, the lemon sky changing to soft blue... How long had Gilles been gone—how long before he was back? Hurry, she had to hurry!

Hardly knowing what she was doing, she flung herself across the room, snatched up the phone and dialled reception. 'Can I speak to Mr Mark Thompson, please? No, I'm sorry—I don't know his room number.'

Perhaps Mark had left already. In which case... 'Hello.' Mark's voice, slightly breathless. She was still rehearsing a careful speech, but found herself instead blurting out, 'It's me—Vicki Summers. Look, are you still getting the early flight?'

'I was planning to.' The impatience—and the surprise—were barely suppressed. 'I should have left by now—the taxi's outside.'

'Could I——' she swallowed to clear an obstruction in her throat '—could I come with you?'

'Come with me? Well, yes, of course you can, Vicki—if you're ready, that is.'

'And—well, it's a bit awkward,' she felt herself go red with shame, 'but could you possibly buy my ticket? I'll pay you back as soon as we're home, I promise. I'll give you a——'

'Sure I will. Don't give it another thought.' Beneath the reassurance, the curiosity was almost crackling down the line.

'Oh, thanks, Mark.' She could have wept with relief. 'And don't worry,' as he tried to speak, 'I'll see you downstairs in just a few minutes.'

She slammed the receiver down, then almost ran through into the bathroom. Her body ached slightly and she would have loved a hot, soaking bath, but there was no time even for a shower. Instead, she splashed her face and hands in the sketchiest of washes, scrubbed at her teeth and dragged the comb through her dishevelled hair, trying not to notice her face, the eyes dark, the mouth swollen from the passion of Gilles' kisses.

He had loaned her a small case and she tugged it out of the wardrobe, seeing the gilt letters G H L embossed in the brown leather. She'd asked him what the H stood for and he'd pulled a face, saying that it was for Henri, after his great-grandfather... She opened it, pulled off her nightie, and threw it in. He must have picked up the black dress, for it lay over a chair, together with the ivory bra and pants and the grey silk nightdress.

For a second she faltered, feeling again the sweet pain of last night, then bundled them up, together with the turquoise dress and the remaining underwear, and thrust them all in. She would keep everything that he had given her; hot tears pricked at her eyes as she felt a sudden, overwhelming need to take with her these—what?—tangible memories? She had no time to seek for reasons now. She would repay him, as she'd vowed, but she could not bear to leave them here in this impersonal hotel-room for Gilles to find when he came back.

She put on Monique's old bra and pants and dragged on the apricot dress and jacket. For a heart-stopping moment, when she snapped open her bag, she couldn't see her new passport. Surely Gilles hadn't——? No, it was there, wedged in the mirror compartment. She ran her fingers through her hair to smooth it down, swung the bag on to her shoulder and picked up the case.

Once outside her room, she made for the fire exit sign at the end of the corridor. She dared not use the lift or the main stairs—Gilles might have finished his meeting and at this very moment be returning to their floor. She skittered down the plain concrete stairs, emerged at the side of the building and raced round to the front entrance where Mark was pacing up and down beside a blue Peugeot cab, its engine revving.

With no time for words, he pushed her and her case into the back seat, leapt in beside her, and they both sank back into the soft upholstery as the cab pulled away through the gardens, past the ranks of guests' cars. Among them she glimpsed a peacock-blue Renault Alpine, then they were out through the hotel gates and into the morning traffic.

CHAPTER ELEVEN

'VICKI? Andy here—Andy Lennox. Hi, how are you?'

'Andy! Hello. I'm fine, thanks.'

'Where have you been? We've been trying to reach you for days.'

'Sorry. I've just got back from Sydney—in fact, I've only just this second walked in through the front door.' Vicki realised that she was still clutching her heavy case from when she had snatched up the ringing phone, and she set it down. 'I've been out there interviewing three of the stars of that new soap that's taking off.'

'Great. Working as hard as ever, then. Still freelancing, are you?'

'Yes. I prefer it, actually.'

'I liked that piece of yours in the colour supplement the other week. Great stuff—you really peeled off the layers there. Anyway, what I'm ringing about is—remember that proposal you put up, oh, way back, last September? You know, your idea about that village in France—Montaillou. We—A.J. shelved it at the time——'

Shelved it? Vicki permitted herself a wry smile. That was one way of putting the reception her proposal had received from Adrian Jones, Andy's—and her one-time—boss at the Small Screen video and film-making company. Still, as it happened, it hadn't mattered—not with Mark making definite that job offer even before they'd landed at Heathrow.

'Well, we've got a new series planned. It's about women—their roles through the ages, et cetera, et cetera.' She caught the faintly ironic note in his voice. 'They want a sociological slant, and off-beat with it—none of your Mary Queen of Scots and Florence Nightingale. Strictly minority viewing, no doubt, although we can but hope, I suppose—we're aiming to hype it up a bit. Anyway, we think one programme could be built around that mistress of the château that you told us about, Béatrice Whatsername.'

'De Planissoles.'

'Yes, well, she sounds as if she was a bit of a mediaeval little raver—quite a girl, in fact.'

Quite a girl... Vicki winced involuntarily, as though she'd bitten on a bad tooth. Just for a moment, she heard Gilles' sardonic voice uttering those very words. It had been the evening after her abortive flight into the mountains, when she'd told him about her plans and he'd insisted on her doing the brochure...

'We thought we'd get a young unknown actress to play her—fun and games in the fourteenth-century haystacks and all that. The castle's ruined, I gather, but you'll be able to find another one nearby for the interiors, no doubt.'

'Me?'

'Yes. A.J. wants you to go back down there—look out some likely locations. He'd like you to come in and talk about it.'

Vicki almost dropped the phone. Go back to Montaillou, she thought dazedly, hardly more than a few crow's miles across the mountains from that other valley—Gilles' valley—which she'd left more than six months before? There had been times since when she had almost come to believe that he had cast a shadow on her life forever. Her work on his brochure had been engrossing, and yet the identical kind of work for Mark's company had very quickly palled into boredom. In the end, she had been forced to admit, though she had fought angrily against the realisation, that it was the brochure's owner rather than the brochure itself that had worked such a spell of fascination over her... At least that was all now safely behind her. But if she were to go back...

Poor Mark. She felt the old stab of guilt. His devotion had left her quite unmoved—desperately wanting to return his growing feelings for her, yet numbed inside, she was totally unable to do so. Finally, that evening when he'd asked her, almost angrily, to marry him, and she'd refused as gently as she could, he had said, 'It's that bloody Frenchman—Laroque—still, isn't it?'

'Gilles? Oh, no, Mark, you're quite wrong. It's—it's just that——' She had floundered, then faltered into silence, and he'd picked up her words.

'It's just that you can't even *see* anyone else, let alone fall for them.' That's not true, she'd tried to protest, but her words had died away.

After that, she'd given in her notice and hurled herself into a frenzy of work, freelancing first for trade journals, then for several women's magazines. She'd surprised herself how well she'd done. It was as though her confidence, all but shattered, had bounced back, and now there were more offers of work than she could really cope with. Still, that was how she liked it: always busy, no time to sit and think. In fact, over the next few months, she'd discovered that it was quite easy, really, to blot something out—if you were determined enough, that was. Work could easily expand to fill every waking moment of the day—and sometimes even the night.

A week after she'd arrived back in England, a stiff brown manilla envelope with a French stamp and familiar handwriting had arrived. She'd opened it with unsteady hands and out had tumbled a fat wad of brand new English banknotes. She'd stared at them stupidly for several seconds, then tipped up the envelope for the letter, but there was no letter. Nothing, just that impersonal bundle of ten-pound notes—far too much for the work she'd done.

When at last, days before she left for Australia, she had saved up enough in her bank account, she had sent Gilles—not money, but a cheque for all her clothes, with extra to cover his overpayment. After much agonising, she had enclosed a rather stilted little note, simply hoping that he was well...

Dimly, from far away, she heard Andy's voice. 'Right, Van, I'm coming,' then, 'That's OK, is it, Vicki, ten-thirty on Wednesday? Great, we're all looking forward to seeing you again. Bye.'

'Bye.'

Mechanically, Vicki put down the phone. Oh, well, it wouldn't hurt to go in, although with the end of the month deadline for her Oz interviews she really ought to get stuck into them. Still, it would be nice to see Andy and the others again. They'd all been very worried about her, and now they'd be able to see just how well she was.

Her post was lying in a tumbled heap just behind the door, where she had heard the phone ringing and had run up the last few steps, dragging her luggage with her. She picked it up and went through to the kitchen, leafing idly through it as she went. There was enough, considering she'd only been away a week. Gas bill...circulars...letter with an Edinburgh postmark—that would be Libby, her old schoolfriend...more circulars...and—her hands went very still—a letter with a French stamp, her name and address typed.

With trembling fingers she ripped open the envelope and took out her cheque, now torn in half. Nothing else. She stood holding the small pieces of paper and stared down at them, trying to puzzle out what they were doing there. Her brain was refusing to function; the jet lag of nearly thirty hours' travel must be catching up with her.

Then her face crumpled as though she were in pain. With a convulsive gesture she screwed up the remains of the cheque, and dropped them into her pedal-bin.

She filled the kettle to make herself a pot of tea, and while it was boiling switched on the central heating—although it was early May, the flat felt quite chilled—then she stood, outwardly impassive, leaning against the small pine table, arms folded, her fingers tapping against them.

The kitchen units were covered with a fine layer of dust. She straightened up and drew a finger across her beautiful old Welsh dresser, wrinkling her nose in disgust. Later, when she'd had a rest and something to eat, she really must clean the flat before getting stuck into her notes and taped interviews. As for all her china—she smiled faintly as her eye wandered over the dresser shelves, loaded with the pretty cups, plates and dishes which she'd been collecting from antique stalls for the last few months—although she'd washed them all just before she'd left, they needed doing again. Perhaps later this evening...she really ought to shop for food, though—she didn't appear to have left much in her fridge-freezer.

The kettle boiled, she made a pot of tea, found an opened packet of ginger biscuits which weren't too soft, and went through to the small, neat living-room. In her diary, she entered her appointment: 'Wednesday, 10.30, Montaillou,' then she sat frowning at it. How strange. It had been so vivid: Béatrice de Planissoles, the priest Pierre Clergue, Pierre Maury and the other shepherds, all living, breathing people. Now, they were faded into grey, insubstantial shadows . . .

If she was going to get involved in this programme about them she was going to have to psych herself up, recreate them in her mind—and before Wednesday. But would she be able to do that? Did she want to? Could she ever bring herself even to face the thought of returning to France—and to that part of France in particular?

'Dear girl, how good to see you again.'

'Hello, Adrian.' Vicki smiled at her ex-boss. Was she imagining it, or was there just a shade more warmth in A.J.'s manner towards her?

'Apologies for receiving you in the cutting-room, Vicki,' he waved an elegant hand around the rather cramped studio, 'but we're just finishing off an editing session. Be with you soon. You know everybody, don't you?'

'Oh, yes.' Vicki gave a quick smile to the small group of her former colleagues, gathered around the editing machine with its twin screens, then slid into a chair that Adrian pulled out for her next to a pretty brunette. 'Hi, Van, how are you?'

Vanessa winked at her with the eye furthest from her employer, then said, 'Hi, Vicki. Great to see you again.'

'We're checking through a promotional video we're making for the EEC—their agricultural policy section,' Adrian was going on. 'Hardly of riveting interest, Vicki, but still, if you'll pardon the phrase, work like this is our bread and butter—literally, in this case.'

Vicki smiled obediently at the little joke; everyone else merely looked glazed.

'Right, Derek, let's get on. Where were we? Oh yes, Holland.'

The editor restarted the twin tapes and on to the screens came shots of lush watermeadows, cows grazing peacefully in the shadow of what looked like a toy windmill, an arrow-straight canal running away into the distance.

'Hmm, bit heavy, this, even for our agricultural friends. Could do with some music, perhaps. Nothing too taxing, of course.'

'How about gems from *The Flying Dutchman*?' Van's voice whispered in Vicki's ear and she grinned, relaxing back into her chair. She'd forgotten how good it felt to be part of a close-knit team. Maybe that was all that was wrong with her: why, in spite of all her interesting work, she so often felt listless, why sometimes it was almost too much trouble even to open a tin of baked beans for herself. She'd been on her own so much lately—by choice, of course, but even so...

The pastures of Holland faded into a brilliantly colourful sequence of hectares of sunflower plants in full bloom—presumably destined to end up in tubs of polyunsaturated margarine... Yes, it really was just like old times. Perhaps she *would* take on the Montaillou programme. After all, she really couldn't spend the rest of her life avoiding a country twenty miles away across the English Channel—that would be just too childish.

The sunflowers were replaced by a row of mountains, their jagged peaks slashing the skyline. Vicki tensed in her chair, her eyes dilating with shock. It couldn't be——

'Ah, you'll find this section more interesting, Vicki.' Adrian was leaning across to her. 'It's near where you were, I think. We could maybe even use some of this footage for your programme.'

She did not turn her head, but sat rigid, her eyes fixed on the small, flickering screens. The camera was panning down now past ranks of pine trees—the scene so vivid that she could almost smell their tangy scent—to rolling pastures filled with hundreds—no, thousands of milling sheep, all pouring down from the mountainside.

Behind them were a dozen or so men on horseback. The camera slowly zoomed in towards one of them, a big man who sat astride his horse with an easy grace, reining it in as its hoofs skittered, drawing sparks on the steep, uneven track. His face was in the shadow cast by a wide-brimmed hat, and yet—Vicki stared hungrily at the screens, as though she wanted to devour the film.

'That's the boss.' Very small and far away, as though from the far end of a tunnel, she heard Andy's voice. 'I've met some awkward customers in my time, but that one beats anybody. He was a real bastard. What was his name?'

'Laroque—Gilles Laroque, wasn't it?' Van put in beside her. 'A bastard, maybe, but man, was he gorgeous!' Vicki, all her senses straining, felt the girl smile to herself, and instantly she tensed against the wholly irrational desire to leap from her seat and fall on her unwitting friend. 'But there was nothing doing there, I'm afraid,' Vanessa sighed regretfully.

'You bet there wasn't, Van.' Andy laughed. 'He's way out of your league, darling. Lord of the bloody valley, he is, and doesn't he know it? Do you know, Vicki, he can speak perfect English, but he just didn't choose to when we were around? We did an interview with him, and we're going to have to dub that because the arrogant swine insisted on speaking French.'

'Wh——' Vicki swallowed and tried again. 'When were you there?'

'Oh, the end of last year. October, wasn't it, Van? They were bringing the sheep down for the winter. We stayed on and filmed in the village that night. They were having a sort of all-night party——'

'A *fête*.' Vicki heard her own voice, tight against her throat.

'That's it. Look, it's coming up now.'

It was evening, the trees in the small square twinkling with coloured fairy lights, trestle tables laden with food, a band in one corner. There was Jeanne's *auberge*; that window on the far right was her bedroom—the room where she had first seen that stranger with those hostile eyes which had so chilled her. There were people, people everywhere—and there he was, moving among the dancers.

She screwed up her eyes, though whether to see more clearly or against the shocking suddenness of the pain which hit her she wasn't sure. Like all the others, he was wearing traditional costume—or so it appeared: straight black trousers and black knee boots, a white shirt and a fitted black jacket, which seemed moulded to his powerful body, topped by a wide-brimmed, almost Spanish-looking hat.

He moved among the revellers, smiling, talking, shaking hands, and yet Vicki, her senses yearning towards him with every fibre of her being, could see that his movements were those of an automaton, as though he was playing no real part in the merry-making—as though everything except his physical body was a very long way away.

Now, through the swirl of dancers, she could glimpse him sitting at one of the trestle tables talking to a group of old men—his former shepherds, perhaps. He was holding a glass of wine, but she could see his fingers merely toying with it, circling it round and round. He was clearly unaware that the camera was on him, and at the sight of his face, half obscured as it was, a sombre, brooding mask, she felt as though an icy hand was slowly squeezing her heart——

'OK. That's enough of these bucolic jollifications. Derek, can you cut to the interview section?'

'Sure.'

The remainder of the *fête* sequence sped through at breakneck speed, then the pictures slowed and the screens displayed a shot of the house, with an unsmiling Gilles in the foreground, speaking directly to the camera.

'See what I mean?' breathed Andy, as Gilles outlined in rapid, uncompromising French the various aspects of his enterprises—the quality of the wool, the international market for his fabrics, the move into cheese products... His voice—Gilles' voice! How strained he looked, how haggard... He must have been ill, not long after she'd left—and if this was last October, how was he now?

'Can you hold it there, Derek?' The image in full close-up of Gilles' face froze on the screens, the indigo-blue eyes seeming to stare straight at Vicki. 'We're going to have to break this up—keep the voice-over going but feed in something of what he's talking about. Any ideas, Andy?'

'Well, we've got some footage of that bloody great ram of his. What was it called?'

'Casanova!' Vicki didn't realise she'd spoken until they all turned to look at her in surprise.

'That's it. But how—Vicki, are you all right?'

She had leapt to her feet. That icy hand was gripping her heart even more tightly and her breath was coming in short, wrenching gasps. She had to get out of this overheated room, away from these people who were all looking up at her, frozen into attitudes of astonishment and concern. They think I'm having another breakdown, she thought, but what does it matter? What does anything matter?

'Come on through to my office, Vicki. I'll get you a drink, then we can talk about your programme——'

'No—no, thank you, A.J.' Somehow, she had retrieved her voice. 'I'm sorry, but there's something I must do. I'll be in touch. Bye.'

She flashed everyone and no one a brilliant smile, snatched up her bag and fled.

At the bottom of the street she leaned against a wall until her shaking legs began to feel as though they belonged to her again. She closed her eyes, desperately trying to blot out that face, but it was no use—stern, unsmiling, it danced up and down behind her tight-closed lids. And she knew the truth. It had taken just the flickering images on those screens to show her that the feelings she'd had for Gilles, which she'd tried—how she'd tried—to bury under an edifice of non-stop work and pretty china, were still there and would not go away.

She had to go to him, if only to see if he really had been—was still—ill. But how would he receive her—after she'd fled from him without a word? That cheque . . . torn in two . . . She winced at the thought of how he would meet her. He would no doubt tell her to get the hell out of his valley, out of his life, but it was no use—she had to go to him.

CHAPTER TWELVE

EVERYTHING looked the same. Only the deep greens and browns of the trees and fields had been replaced by the soft, fresh shades of early May. There was the gateway where those two young men had so politely but firmly barred her way when, in her blind terror of Gilles, she had fled from the house. She permitted herself a brief, wry smile as she drove past. Maybe a little spot of healthy terror might be useful just now, for who could predict how that most unpredictable of men would receive her this time?

And yet, within her, she could only feel a surging gladness that made her, almost without realising it, depress the accelerator pedal harder and harder as she drove through the village, every house shuttered, as they had been that other time, but now against the warmth of the spring afternoon.

As she rounded the final bend, the old, sprawling stone house was facing her. On her way from Toulouse she'd hoped, in her feverish anxiety, that Gilles would be there—she needed to see him quickly, before she had time to regret her precipitate action of the previous day. But it was the housekeeper, Madame Duval, who answered her tentative knock.

'Mademoiselle Summers!' Was Vicki imagining it, or was there, behind the surprise, a barely hidden gleam of pleasure—or even relief? 'No, Monsieur Gilles is not here—he is up in the pastures.'

Well, of course, where else would he be? Vicki refused the offer of coffee; she was thirsty after the flight and the hair-raising trip up from Toulouse, but something inside her was urging her on, driving her towards Gilles.

She kept to the car for as long as possible, but then, when the track became too steep and rocky, she edged gingerly on to the narrow verge and stopped. The sun was hot on her bare arms, the turquoise dress clammy on her back. Although fearful of its likely effect on Gilles, she'd consciously chosen to wear it for some reason, but it really was too warm. She should have spared just five minutes at the house to change. She hesitated, then hauled out from the case on the seat behind her a blouse in peach voile and a white linen wrap-over skirt, and quickly changed into them.

It was a long, tiring climb and she was glad of the dense, blue-grey shade of the pines, but at last she reached the pastures. The lush meadows were overflowing with sheep and lambs and the air was filled with their pathetic, insistent bleatings. And yes, just as Gilles had said, the ground was a carpet of deep yellow buttercups, the whole scene even more lovely than he had told her.

She walked through the field, almost knee-deep in the burnished gold flowers, rounded a crumbling stone wall which must once have been part of a byre or a shepherd's hut, then stopped abruptly. Ahead of her were several men, and among them, kneeling over a shapeless woolly bundle, was Gilles.

His back was to her and she had to cling on to the wall suddenly against the intoxicating surge of painful rapture which left her weak and trembling. Her slight movement sent some of the sheep shying nervously across the field, and one of the shepherds, glancing up, saw her. He muttered something and she saw Gilles go very still for an instant, then, without turning even fractionally in her direction, he went on with what he was doing. He lifted the new-born lamb, set it on its tiny black hooves and gave it a gentle push which sent it staggering unsteadily to the ewe.

Only then did he slowly straighten up and turn to look at her. Then he was coming towards her, rolling down the sleeves of his blue shirt as he approached.

She had tried to brace herself for anger, recriminations—for anything he chose to hurl at her—but there was—*nothing*, just the cold aloofness of a forbidding stranger. He stood regarding her, his thumbs resting in the belt of his jeans, seemingly completely at ease, although she could see the taut, compressed lines of his mouth and sense the tensions coiling inside him.

'H-hello, Gilles. How are you?' Stupid question—but she had to say something to break this silence, even though her voice sounded so tight and unnatural.

But still he did not speak, only looked at her, his eyes chips of glacial ice, seeming hardly to see her. Vicki, her shoulders sagging wearily, was grateful for her sunglasses to hide the misery which otherwise must surely be revealed to his contemptuous gaze. She ached to touch him, hold him, say over and over again, I'm sorry, Gilles, I'm sorry. Please take me in your arms as you did that night, but this frozen-eyed stranger was freezing her, too. She should never have come, she should have stayed a million miles away, struggling to conquer her feelings once again, to suffocate under a blanket of overwork her love for this hard, unyielding man.

'Why the hell have you come here?'

His voice pierced her like cold steel, and she flinched, bunching her fingers in her skirt pockets as she fought down the urge to cover her ears and run away, back to her car, back to the oblivion of England. But somehow she had to keep from him the knowledge of just how much he was hurting her, for that would merely feed his contempt.

'Oh.' She forced a careless shrug. 'I was passing this way. I'm doing that Montaillou programme, after all, so I thought I'd——'

'And how is Thompson?'

'Mark?' This was one question she had not prepared herself for. 'He's fine—at least, he was the last time I saw him.' Of course, he was really talking about her running away. 'Look, Gilles, I can explain—about that morning, I mean.'

'Explain! What is there to explain? You went off with him. No——' as she went to interrupt '—do not try to lie. The receptionist saw him handing you into a cab, and further informed me that you had rung his room ten minutes previously. You had no money, so he clearly paid your air fare—although you have, no doubt, amply recompensed him by now.' There was open anger coupled with the contempt in his voice now and he swept her gasp of furious protest aside. 'And I also know that you have been working for him since you returned to London.'

'How—you've been *spying* on me!' He lifted his shoulders in a careless shrug and she jutted her chin fiercely. 'But I'm afraid I've got news for you. Your spies, whoever they are, are not that efficient. I left Mark's firm months ago, and haven't seen him since. And as for that morning—no——' it was her turn now to brush aside his attempt at interruption '—you must listen to me. I know how it must have seemed, but——'

'Do you, Victoria?' A dusky flush was now tinging his cheekbones. 'I wonder if you do. I came back to your room, to find that you had gone—vanished, without a single word.'

She felt the guilt show on her face. She'd wanted, even in her haste, to scribble at least a line, but somehow no words came, and nothing had seemed preferable to anything. Miserably unable to meet his accusing eyes, she lowered her gaze to the ground.

'I'm s-sorry, Gilles. I am, truly,' she whispered, so softly that he had to strain to hear her. 'It was wrong of me, I know, but it was just—oh, what's the use?' She broke off as her voice quivered. 'I shouldn't have come.'

She turned away but, before she could take more than two stumbling steps, Gilles' hand had snatched hold of her arm.

'No, Vicki——'

The sound of cheerful, unnaturally loud whistling broke in on his words. The shepherds, dogs at heel, were walking away down the field, studiously avoiding looking in their direction. Gilles grimaced, but at the same time she felt some of the tension run out of him.

'Come—this way.' His hand still tightly on her arm, he steered her the opposite way. 'We must talk.'

Vicki smiled uncertainly at him. 'That's what you said in your note—we must talk.'

'Yes, well,' his voice was still grim, 'this time we shall.'

Behind the ruined byre a huge black horse, loosely haltered to a fallen tree-trunk, was idly nipping at the tops of the meadow grasses. He whinnied softly as they approached, and Gilles clicked his tongue at him. Releasing the bridle, he swung himself up into the saddle and then, before Vicki could protest, he had caught her up and perched her precariously side-saddle in front of him, before beginning to steer the horse up the hillside.

Vicki glanced down for a moment; the tallest buttercups were a long way below her. She gasped and made an involuntary clutch at Gilles' shirt-front and he put one arm around her, pulling her to him so that, just as on that crazy, mind-tingling motorbike ride down the mountainside months before, she was conscious of the hard, muscled power of his body, of the warm smell which was Gilles—a mixture of sweat, the open air and soap—and which compounded in her brain to make her senses reel with her awareness of the nearness of him.

'Why have you come?'

The same question, if more mildly put, and she still hedged. 'Well, the company that's making this Montaillou programme, they made that promotional film you were in. I saw it—recently.' Yesterday morning, to be exact... Had it really just been yesterday?

'Hmm.' Gilles gave a rueful laugh. 'I seem to remember that I was not very—co-operative on that occasion.'

'No, that was the impression I got.'

'You know,' he went on thoughtfully, 'there seems to be something about the English that brings out the worst in me.'

'Yes, you may be right there,' she replied demurely, keeping her eyes firmly on the third button of his blue cotton shirt.

They rode on in silence for some minutes, then, 'Why did you go, Vicki?' His breath stirred the fine hairs at her forehead, but she could not turn to him. 'You must surely have known how I felt about you.'

'Yes, you pitied me,' she said flatly, still avoiding his gaze. 'You felt sorry for me—my pathetic little story—what a total, utter failure I'd been.' The jerky, disconnected phrases tumbled out. Since she'd left Bordeaux, she'd scarcely given David—or her life with him—a single thought, yet now her lips twisted in a spasm of that remembered anguish.

'I couldn't stand your pity,' she went on fiercely. 'It was worse than all your anger, your contempt. I—I couldn't bear it.'

Her fingers were twisting and untwisting in her lap, until he caught them up in his hands.

'And yet,' he said softly, 'that night, I allowed you to pity me—for Claudia. For the first time, I let someone show me compassion, and I accepted it.'

She wanted to say, Yes, but you're bigger, stronger than me, in every way, but the words stuck fast and he went on, 'Vicki, I did pity you, it is true. But you must know that pity is the least of what I feel for you.'

He paused for her reply, but something in his voice was doing strange things to her breathing, clamping on to her lungs so that she could not speak.

'Why do you think I dreamed up those reasons to keep you here? As I told you, I quickly realised that you were completely innocent in the affair at the *auberge*, and you were right, of course, I had no rèal need of you at Bordeaux—except that in my mind and body I had every need for you.'

A tremor was running through her but she forced herself to stay silent as he went on. 'I was determined that you would not go. I would bring you, by force if necessary, back to the valley with me. I wanted to have you lie in my bed all night, then fold you in a sheepskin wrap and hold you in my arms to watch the sun come up over the mountains. But instead—you ran away.'

He put his hand beneath her chin, knuckling her head up so that she was now forced to meet his eyes, blue-black with suppressed anger. 'I loved you, Vicki.' He shook his head, in fierce impatience at his own weakness. 'And, damn you, I love you still.'

Gilles loved her! Joy—incredible joy at his words was surging through her. 'But why——' she could hardly get the words out '—why didn't you come after me? Why didn't you come to London, instead of sending me all that money, like some horrible blood-money payment?'

'Pourquoi?' Gilles spread one hand, palm up in a telling gesture. 'You had gone with Thompson. I realised that there must have been more between you than you were prepared to admit, and besides——' He stopped, a note of uncertainty in his voice for the first time.

'Besides?' she prompted.

'I was racked by guilt. After all, I had all but—raped you.'

Quite unable to bear the bruised look of self-disgust in his eyes, she said quickly, 'Oh, Gilles, no, you didn't.' She smiled through the hot tears of happiness that were burning her eyelids. 'That night—I wanted you to make love to me. There—there was nothing of rape in what you did. You see, I loved you, and——' her tearful smile took on an almost teasing pout '—damn you, I love you still!'

'Oh, Vicki.'

She heard him draw in his breath, then his arms went round her, straining her to him, and he buried his head in her hair in a long, motionless embrace until the horse, bored with standing still, snorted and tossed his head impatiently.

'All right, Carlos, boy.' Keeping a firm hold of Vicki with one hand, Gilles seized the reins with the other, touched the horse's flanks and they trotted off, still heading upwards.

At last he slowed beside a fast-running stream, dismounted, then lifted her off Carlos' back, sliding her very slowly down against his body. As he knotted the reins, she looked about her. It was the same stream, the same place where she'd crossed, then fallen, bringing Gilles down beside her.

Today, under the shadowy trees, the grass was thickly starred with small mauve orchids and the water was higher, lapping over the precarious rock steps, but he caught her up in his arms and strode across, more sure-footed than he had been that other time.

He set her down, still locked within the circle of his arms, the strong beat of his heart pounding under her spread hands, and they stared into each other's eyes with almost greedy avidity. As he bent over her, her lips opened to him and his honeyed sweetness filled her mouth so that she gave a muffled moan and closed her eyes, clenching her hands on his shoulders, her nails digging through the rough cotton of his shirt.

Dimly, she was aware that they had sunk to their knees; he was unbuttoning her blouse, sliding it away from her shoulders, then releasing the waistband of her skirt, but very slowly, as though to reassure her that this time would be different. He held her away from him to pull her free of her clothes and she heard his harsh breath, saw his eyes glitter, as he revealed the ivory lingerie which he had given her.

As he unhooked the tiny bra and slid her out of the wisp of panties, his hands were shaking and she sensed the ruthless control with which he was reining in his desire. Lost now to everything but her yearning need for him, she went to pull him to her again, but he trapped her slender wrists with one hand and raised them to his lips.

'Gently, my little one. Be patient.' It was a throaty murmur against her heated skin as he lowered her gently down to the yielding grass.

Still keeping hold of her wrists, he let his eyes travel over her slender body, the high line of her breasts, the flat, creamy smoothness of her stomach, in a voyage of slow discovery almost more voluptuous than a hand's touch would have been.

'If you knew how much I have wanted to see you like this—ever since that morning when I first set eyes on you.' His voice was very low, and she knew that he was speaking to himself as much as to her. 'That first time, when I held you in my arms to carry you from the *auberge*, I could hardly restrain myself from tearing that flimsy nightdress from you. And then, when I brought you to my house, I felt ashamed—as though I was violating your unconscious body with the strength of my desire to possess you.'

He gave her a wry half-smile, then went on huskily, 'I had to take refuge in anger—with you, and with myself. I suppose I could not bear that another woman—even a woman so different—should have such power over me, so I forced myself to fight against my weakness.'

This hard man was yielding to her, paying homage to her body, opening his soul to her. Vicki trembled inside at the knowledge of the weapon he had put in her hands, should she choose to use it.

Then, as he lowered his head and very softly kissed the tender, quivering flesh of her inner thigh, she gave a shudder. His lips, his hands, his voice, the potent male scent of him, all were conspiring to set her alight, kindling the dry tinder within her to blazing heat. Her senses were sending a message to every palpitating nerve-ending of her body, telling her that she was hungry—*starving* for the assuagement that only he could give.

'Please, Gilles.'

It was a low moan, then she was dragging with fumbling urgency at his shirt, freeing it from his belt, sliding her hands up inside to fasten on the moist flesh of his back.

'Please, Gilles,' she whispered again, and this time he stood up, shedding his clothes with a silent intentness which in another life might have terrified her. Now, though, she watched through half-closed eyes until he stood over her, naked, his face, his body both now revealing to her the potency of his desire.

As he had done to her, now she slowly surveyed his body, her eyes sliding across the bronzed satin-sheen skin. Nothing had prepared her for such beauty. Jeans, dungarees, even the well-cut suits he had worn in Bordeaux, they had all masked the superb animal perfection, the proudly set head, the breadth of shoulders, the powerful thighs and buttocks.

'You're so—*beautiful*,' she said in wonderment, and Gilles gave a low, throaty purr like a panther.

'And so are you, my darling—and very desirable, as you must be very well aware.'

In times past, she would have blushed scarlet at the clear meaning in his words. Now, though, she opened her arms and he came down into them, his urgency pressing her into the lush, orchid-starred grass. This time, as he'd promised, it was all sweetness, his power not hurting her but sending shafts of feelings through her so exquisite that they were a kind of delicious anguish exploding in tiny bursts of white-hot fire through her whole body so that she cried out aloud, burying her teeth in his shoulder.

'No—Vicki,' he gasped against the pulse of her neck, his voice slurred and thickened with his need for her. 'I can't——'

But she whispered against his sweat-soaked skin, 'Yes, yes, yes——' She felt rather than heard his gasp, then his iron control splintered into a million fragments as he was released into a shuddering ecstasy, her body soaring with his until it was a transparent bowl, rapture filling it with golden light.

At last, Gilles raised his head and they smiled at each other, a dazed, rather tremulous smile, as though they had been shaken to the very roots of their being, then he gathered her to him and they lay still...

A long time afterwards he murmured, 'Vicki.'

'Mmm?'

'Marry me.'

Unable to trust her voice, she nodded against him.

'And can you bear to live here?'

Alerted by the undercurrent of anxiety in his voice, she opened her eyes. 'I can't bear to live anywhere without you,' she said simply.

'But the mountains,' he persisted, that crease of uncertainty still between his brows, 'do you still see them as a prison?'

'And you as my forbidding gaoler? No, I don't, Gilles—not any more.' She put up her hand to caress his face, wipe away that furrow, and he caught it, softly pressing the palm to his lips.

The hawthorns were casting long shadows, the sun was almost sinking behind the high peaks, its rays gilding the last few patches of snow which had not yet melted. The mountains... Strange how once she'd thought them menacing, as though they really were that steel-jawed trap waiting to spring. They weren't—not at all. They were a pair of strong, encircling arms...

'What are you thinking, *chérie*?'

She shook her head, smiling to herself. 'Oh, nothing. At least,' she leaned over, snapped off one of the enormous buttercups and lightly brushed it under his chin, 'I was just wondering if you like butter. Hmm—yes, you do—and you know that too much isn't good for you.'

He took hold of her hand, crushing the pollen-yellow petals, then whispered, 'You're right, but I like other things even more—things where too much is *very* good for me.'

'Oh?' Vicki's eyes had a glint of inviting mischief. 'Such as?'

Gilles reached for her. 'Such as this...and this...and this...'

PASSPORT TO ROMANCE VACATION SWEEPSTAKES

OFFICIAL RULES

SWEEPSTAKES RULES AND REGULATIONS. NO PURCHASE NECESSARY.

HOW TO ENTER:

1. To enter, complete this official entry form and return with your invoice in the envelope provided, or print your name, address, telephone number and age on a plain piece of paper and mail to: Passport to Romance, P.O. Box #1397, Buffalo, N.Y. 14269-1397 No mechanically reproduced entries accepted.
2. All entries must be received by the Contest Closing Date, midnight, December 31, 1990 to be eligible
3. Prizes: There will be ten (10) Grand Prizes awarded, each consisting of a choice of a trip for two people to: i) London, England (approximate retail value $5,050 U.S.); ii) England, Wales and Scotland (approximate retail value $6,400 U.S.); iii) Caribbean Cruise (approximate retail value $7,300 U.S.); iv) Hawaii (approximate retail value $ 9,550 U.S.); v) Greek Island Cruise in the Mediterranean (approximate retail value $12,250 U.S.); vi) France (approximate retail value $7,300 U.S.).
4. Any winner may choose to receive any trip or a cash alternative prize of $5,000.00 U.S. in lieu of the trip.
5. Odds of winning depend on number of entries received.
6. A random draw will be made by Nielsen Promotion Services, an independent judging organization on January 29, 1991, in Buffalo, N.Y., at 11:30 a.m. from all eligible entries received on or before the Contest Closing Date. Any Canadian entrants who are selected must correctly answer a time-limited, mathematical skill-testing question in order to win. Quebec residents may submit any litigation respecting the conduct and awarding of a prize in this contest to the Régie des loteries et courses du Quebec.
7. Full contest rules may be obtained by sending a stamped, self-addressed envelope to: "Passport to Romance Rules Request", P.O. Box 9998, Saint John, New Brunswick, E2L 4N4.
8. Payment of taxes other than air and hotel taxes is the sole responsibility of the winner.
9. Void where prohibited by law.

- -

PASSPORT TO ROMANCE VACATION SWEEPSTAKES

OFFICIAL RULES

SWEEPSTAKES RULES AND REGULATIONS. NO PURCHASE NECESSARY.

HOW TO ENTER:

1. To enter, complete this official entry form and return with your invoice in the envelope provided, or print your name, address, telephone number and age on a plain piece of paper and mail to: Passport to Romance, P.O. Box #1397, Buffalo, N.Y. 14269-1397. No mechanically reproduced entries accepted.
2. All entries must be received by the Contest Closing Date, midnight, December 31, 1990 to be eligible.
3. Prizes: There will be ten (10) Grand Prizes awarded, each consisting of a choice of a trip for two people to: i) London, England (approximate retail value $5,050 U.S.); ii) England, Wales and Scotland (approximate retail value $6,400 U.S.); iii) Caribbean Cruise (approximate retail value $7,300 U.S.); iv) Hawaii (approximate retail value $ 9,550 U.S.); v) Greek Island Cruise in the Mediterranean (approximate retail value $12,250 U.S.); vi) France (approximate retail value $7,300 U.S.).
4. Any winner may choose to receive any trip or a cash alternative prize of $5,000.00 U.S. in lieu of the trip.
5. Odds of winning depend on number of entries received.
6. A random draw will be made by Nielsen Promotion Services, an independent judging organization on January 29, 1991, in Buffalo, N.Y., at 11:30 a.m. from all eligible entries received on or before the Contest Closing Date. Any Canadian entrants who are selected must correctly answer a time-limited, mathematical skill-testing question in order to win. Quebec residents may submit any litigation respecting the conduct and awarding of a prize in this contest to the Régie des loteries et courses du Quebec.
7. Full contest rules may be obtained by sending a stamped, self-addressed envelope to: "Passport to Romance Rules Request", P.O. Box 9998, Saint John, New Brunswick, E2L 4N4.
8. Payment of taxes other than air and hotel taxes is the sole responsibility of the winner.
9. Void where prohibited by law

 RLS-DIR

PASSPORT TO ROMANCE
WIN 1 of 10 Vacations SEE INSIDE

VACATION SWEEPSTAKES

MONTH 2 ENTRY

Official Entry Form

Yes, enter me in the drawing for one of ten Vacations-for-Two! If I'm a winner, I'll get my choice of any of the six different destinations being offered — and I won't have to decide until after I'm notified!

Return entries with invoice in envelope provided along with Daily Travel Allowance Voucher. Each book in your shipment has two entry forms — and the more you enter, the better your chance of winning!

Name

Address Apt.

City State/Prov. Zip/Postal Code

Daytime phone number ______ Area Code

☐ I am enclosing a Daily Travel Allowance Voucher in the amount of $______ Write in amount revealed beneath scratch-off